In the
Dragon's
Shadow
After the Rain

Printed in Australia

Cover and internal design by Shawline Publishing Group Pty Ltd

Images within this book are copyright approved for Shawline Publishing Group Pty Ltd

First printing: March 2024

Shawline Publishing Group Pty Ltd

www.shawlinepublishing.com.au

Paperback ISBN 978-1-9231-0145-6

eBook ISBN 978-1-9231-0146-3

Hardback ISBN 978-1-9231-0186-9

Distributed by Shawline Distribution and Lightning Source Global

 A catalogue record for this work is available from the National Library of Australia

In The Dragon's Shadow

After The Rain

Rufin De Villiers

Also by Rufin de Villiers

In the Dragon's Shadow series
Absolution

Dedicated to my family and friends

Chapter I

The Status Quo

It was all a dull drone in his ears. There were so many people. There were always so many people. It was something he thought he'd become accustomed to. He was not.

He took a moment, needing some time to realign. He stood against the wall of a tall building and watched as the crowds scurried around. Like ants.

The city was vast, the people many, and the noise overwhelming.

After a time, he kicked off the wall and continued on, his destination not much further away. He did not like coming to the city, but he needed to now.

With a tug he fixed the strap of his bag to his shoulder, with another tug he pulled his collar straight. He wore no tie and often got heckled for it, but always found it stifling; there was enough suffocation from other sources, the last struggle should be from his own clothing.

The building in front of him was just as tall as the others around it. His feelings about it and the people inside could be described as indifferent. Nonetheless, it was his destination. He walked inside.

His steps echoed off the walls and once he reached the elevators, he discovered he was not the only one running behind today. She looked at him as he approached, smiling politely as she pressed the button again.

'Good morning.'

He stood adjacent to her but a few feet apart. He had been warned about personal space before.

'Morning,' he responded while stifling a yawn with the back of his hand. 'Train kept you too?'

She smiled at him again and tapped the button twice. 'No,' she returned curtly.

'Catherine, was it?' He leaned a little closer, recognising her but he did not know everyone yet.

Again, she smiled at him and nodded in response, tapping the button a little harder this time. And it surrendered. The lift arrived and she hurried inside. He followed behind her but made sure to keep the designated distance.

The metal carriage rumbled to life and the climb began.

She seemed nervous; he could not understand why. Her dressing seemed fine, neat and smart, quite well kept overall. She had no reason to be anxious.

'What's your name?' she asked suddenly, not looking in his direction.

He decided to remain civil. 'Athrin.' He checked the floor numbers as they whizzed by. 'The new guy.'

She did not say anything else during the trip.

Normally he would be bothered by this – her tone and demeanour seemed off, suddenly asking for his name. But not now, not anymore, he resolved to ignore such things, he resolved to be… civil.

With a beep, the doors opened and she hurried off and disappeared from sight. He wandered out into the open and followed his feet until he reached reception.

A grizzled lady with a bright red perm and long, colourful nails looked up as he approached. 'Morning,' she greeted him past the sound of snapping gum and with a polite-like wave.

'Morning,' he responded friendlily, walking past her and to the back. He crossed through the doors arched with a prevalent 'Staff Only' sign and made his way between the cubicles and the people contained within them. At the far end he reached his designated table and took his seat, needing a moment to settle his thoughts.

The surrounding din was surprisingly quiet given the number of people, the patter of keyboards and clicking of mice, murmured whispers and quietened coughs. It was all so suffocating.

But necessary. There were worse things out there, he knew that, he wouldn't complain and he didn't mind it that much. He was here to do his job. That was the beginning and the end of it.

He pulled a bottle of water from his bag and put it on the table beside him, dropping the bag to the floor. He turned to his desk and was ready for today.

*

A pleasant smell wafted through his senses. It reminded him of the time and he realised how many hours had gone by. It was time for a walk around.

He grabbed the empty bottle and stood, making his way towards the cafeteria where the smell grew stronger, making him hungrier with each step closer. While filling the bottle at the tap, he swept a look around the room. He recognised a few of the people, even remembered some of their names, but no one seemed to notice him yet. Good, easier that way.

When the bottle was topped off, he made his way to the vending machine and perused the various items on display. None of them seemed particularly appetizing, but he was not after sustenance; rather, something closer to a pick-me-up.

'Ah, Athrin. Good, I caught you.'

That did not bode well. He had almost made it half a day without someone 'catching' him. He abandoned the search for sugar and turned to face the man. 'Brent,' he greeted, as politely as he could.

'How is your third week going?' The man was about as tall as Athrin, maybe an inch shorter. He was very well kept, his hair smoothed back and tight to his head. It was clear to Athrin, even before he spoke, how high he held himself. But none of this would bother Athrin; he had resolved to remain civil.

'Going well, thank you.' Athrin beckoned towards the empty chairs; he did not want to create a queue. 'Should we sit?'

'No, no,' he responded quickly, fixing his collar. 'I am far too busy to stay here long.' He looked around for a moment; Athrin could guess why. 'I received an anonymous complaint, you were late today.'

'Right you are, Brent. Will not happen again.'

He raised a hand, a few inches from Athrin's face. 'I don't want to hear your excuses!' he said loudly, attracting the attention of a few wandering ears.

The hand remained there. Right in front of his face. But Athrin chose to ignore it; his resolve was still sturdy.

'Understood,' he said plainly. 'Apologies, Brent.'

He lowered the hand and stood proudly; his authority was fed a healthy meal.

'Good.' He still spoke loudly, seeking to attract the attention. 'And be mindful of other's personal space; I have had some anonymous complaints.'

Athrin could feel a nerve twitch; he hoped it wasn't visible. He began with a nod and only after a moment did he respond. 'Understood.'

The proud peacock nodded and then, with a twirl, strutted off in search of more admiration, carefully slinking from hall to hall to avoid any unnecessary banter lest he overwork himself.

With a somewhat further depleted level of energy, Athrin returned to his desk. Some eyes watched him as he walked, many of those eyes would judge him, but he did not care. He chose to instead remain civil.

*

The elevator hummed all the way down. Athrin watched the receding numbers tick away. He was alone in this small metal box; he preferred it that way – intended it to be this way. Less to worry about.

He left the building, the light from the sunset hidden behind the tall buildings. There were still a lot of people about but less during this time. Again, this was his intent; this was the optimal time for him. He liked the relative solace in the fading light.

The slow walk was calming and allowed reflection; it gave him some time to think and the chance to decompress after the events of each day. He took the long stroll, the walk instead of the transport. He had no pressure to be anywhere. No one was waiting for him.

This was his choice.

A quiet neighbourhood, the odd dog barking in the distance, the stray cry of a domestic quarrel, nothing out of place, everything was normal. It was better this way.

He climbed the metal staircase, one clank at a time. He paced the walkway, one sturdy foot after another. Then he stood in front of the door. For a while he remained there, in silence. His mind afire with thoughts and feelings he hurriedly bottled away. Then he slotted the key, feeling each tumbler give way, and turned the handle to walk inside.

He did not turn on a single light. He did not care for the contents of his bag as he dropped it and his shoes at the threshold. He took a few steps inside and stopped in the centre of the small room. He paused. His resolve was sturdy still.

It was quiet. A distant car on the road, a single rhythmic bark a few houses over, but here inside this small room it was quiet. So very quiet.

This was his choice.

*

'Athrin,' a cheerful voice called. He ignored it. Almost as if he knew better.

'Athrin!' the voice called again. But he resisted. He certainly knew better.

'Athrin!'

He wrenched from his sleep. For a moment he had wavered. He thought he knew better. He had to confirm that he was alone.

His walk was brisk; he had left a little earlier today to meet the new expectations but he wanted to leave nothing to unforeseen circumstances. He was never one for leaving things to chance.

As he walked, he watched the people around him. It was always fascinating to watch them go about their day. They made it look easy, as if they were all on some kind of autopilot, some kind of function he never had access to, or perhaps his was faulty. Effortlessly they queued for coffee, chatted with complete strangers on seemingly equal terms, and then in an instant went about their very different lives. It was fascinating.

That capacity was admirable, he thought.

He joined the crowd in the elevator. The ride up felt longer than usual. Hopefully this would be another normal day. He would try to lie low, as this week already scored an incident.

*

The street lamps clicked on around him as he walked, almost as if guiding his path. It brought his destination into view. A diner – one of the few in this area to be open at this hour and as a result it was one he frequented. He knew some of the people there. Perhaps not by name, but their faces had grown familiar.

'Good evening, honey,' one of those familiar faces greeted him as he entered. There were not many people here, maybe one or two patrons and some staff in the back.

'Evening,' Athrin greeted, taking the seat he always took by the window.

The same woman approached him with a notepad. She scribbled and scratched. 'The regular?'

'Please,' he responded simply.

Without pause, she spun around and yelled some gibberish to the man barely visible in the kitchen.

Athrin's attention returned to the window and the darkened city outside. He let his mind wander; he'd keep the leash tight in hand but allow enough freedom to pass the time.

'Athrin?' a voice pulled him back to reality.

He turned to the speaker, needing a moment to recognise him through the newly adored beard. 'Is that you, Rowley?'

'Sure is!' he cried, taking the seat opposite Athrin without a moment's pause. 'You seem unsure?'

'Well...' Athrin began, pointing to his face with what was almost a smile. 'Are you wearing that thing or is it wearing you?'

'Don't mock it, took ages to grow this splendour.'

'I remember.' He chuckled. 'Peach fuzz.'

'Hey now, that was years ago. Surprised you remember...' He stroked the course river. 'And that's in the problem, ain't it? Haven't seen you in years, Athrin!'

'Has been a while.' He leaned back, taking a quick glance around the room to see if anyone was eavesdropping. Seemed clear. 'What brings you here?'

'Walkin' by,' Rowley began, scratching his neck, 'Spotted you through the window, had to check.'

Something felt off. Athrin put his elbows on the table and leaned ever so slightly forward. 'And now that you have?'

This gave Rowley pause. It did not last long before he laughed it away. 'Relax, Athrin.' He tapped the table with his thumb. 'I'm alone, no motive.'

The feeling remained. But he would try to let it subside. 'Sorry, Rowley.'

'Woah.' He leaned forward to get a better look at Athrin. 'You really did change, huh?'

An eyebrow lifted in response.

'I didn't believe the stories, but it seems some of them might be true.' He shrugged. 'You're still as paranoid though.'

'Cautious.'

'Paranoid!' Rowley laughed some more as he tapped the table again. 'And what's with the getup? You look like an office worker!'

'And you look like a hobo.'

Rowley laughed again. But this time, just before his thumb touched the table, Athrin stopped him with a cold stare. 'Touch the table again and you might lose that hand.'

A little surprised, he met Athrin's eyes. In that moment's pause, they weighed each other. 'That makes me feel like I gotta.'

'I'm not working, Rowley,' he said simply. 'I am out, and I intend to stay out.'

Some time passed, uncomfortable silence between them. The patrons and workers of the diner went about their business, unaware.

Then Rowley waved at the window with the back of his hand. 'That glare. It was enough to end most fights before they started.' He shifted in his seat towards the end then stood. 'Take care, Athrin.'

'You too, Rowley,' he said neutrally, 'I would appreciate it if we did not cross paths again.'

With a nod, Rowley left. Not two moments after he did, the lady approached with Athrin's order, but for some reason his appetite was gone.

*

The room was dark. A cold breeze drifted through to bring some fresh air after being closed up all day. Athrin stood out on the balcony, the tiny space that it was, and stared at the sky. He could only make out a few stars. The speckled veil of the night sky always gave him some measure of solace; it reminded him of the vastness beyond the circumstance.

He could hear the happenings around him. He could always hear it but he ignored it. That was not his concern anymore.

After a while, he smiled to himself. He did not dislike this life. It had come at a cost. His shoulders were weak from the weight he had carried, his eyes dimmer from the life that was, his heart dull and rigid.

Beside him was an ashtray with three buds twisted and squashed, a habit he was never able to kick. He added a fourth to the graveyard before moving it aside. Then he took a deep sigh, felt the cold air enter and exit his lungs, and savoured it. Was this peace, he wondered.

Chapter II

The Cracked Glass

The almost suffocating murmur drowned out his thoughts. It was enough to disturb but not distract, the uncertain balance between indifference and interception. But Athrin was determined to persevere.

He was there, in his cubicle, minding his own business and going through his checklist for today. His bottle of water would not hold out for the remaining list; he would need to run the gauntlet to the kitchen soon.

There was some tapping now. It had tipped the balance towards distracted. He looked up. Brent leaned over the cubicle and tapped on the rail but did not look at Athrin. This continued for a time.

'Athrin,' he began as the tapping intensified. 'Are you busy?'

Athrin alternated between his monitor and Brent a few times. 'Are you?'

'Funny.' The tapping ended with a louder slap. 'Have you seen Catherine?'

He looked around, ending on Brent again. There was no one in the immediate vicinity. 'I have not.'

'Really?'

Athrin looked around again, puzzled. He could not understand this method of conversation, nor could he see the motive. Perhaps he was overthinking it. 'Really.'

Another two taps. Then Brent leaned on the border, resting his chin on the top. It must have been uncomfortable. 'You're a funny man, Athrin.'

'Brent,' he inquired, his curiosity piqued. 'Is there something I can help you with?'

Brent stood quickly, perhaps almost losing his footing, but he recovered and fixed his collar with a fanciful snap. 'No, you've done enough.' Then he trotted off, a slant in his step either from anger or an injury; it was unclear.

Athrin watched him disappear around a corner, still somewhat perplexed, but then continued on with his checklist. Whatever that was, it did not matter.

*

The sun set, the stars came out. Before long, several days had passed. They went by quickly and each without anything of particular interest.

Athrin stood at the elevator. He pushed the button again and stood back, using the time to straighten the strap of his bag. No one was around him; he could have been the last. He tapped the button again, hoping it would help spur it along but knowing it would do nothing.

With a piercing ding it arrived at last, opening slowly. He stepped inside and chose his floor. As the doors started closing, he could hear the hurried pitter-patter of footsteps. Quickly, he grabbed the door and pulled it open, and no sooner did the latecomer hurry inside. He let the doors close and the climb began.

He leaned against the wall, wondering what this day would offer.

'Thank you.' A quiet voice came from behind him.

He peered back and after a moment of searching his memory, connected her face to a name.

'Most welcome,' he told Catherine.

Silence loomed. It meant nothing to him; he preferred it. He had learnt to respond to people, not instigate conversation. It allowed for fewer misunderstandings. Less confrontation.

The elevator rumbled to a halt and the doors inched open. Without pause, she sped from sight, leaving Athrin to stroll leisurely to his desk. He contemplated lunch. Perhaps he would visit the place across the street again.

'Athrin,' a familiar voice snarled.

He stopped and turned to Brent, who was leaning against a wall as if waiting for him.

'Traveling alone today?' he asked Athrin, his grumble audible.

Remain civil. That was the objective. 'I do most days, yes.'

'Hm.' That was louder than it needed to be. And then with a twirl, he robbed Athrin of his presence.

Athrin could guess, and may even be right, but he wasn't here for nonsense. He wanted only to do his part.

*

Athrin neared the end of his checklist. He stretched his shoulders and worked out a few cracks. A glance at the time and he discovered the day was nearly at an end. He was relieved, since the morning the rest of the day had gone uneventful. Until.

'Athrin!'

It was becoming as welcoming as a shrill from a harpy. He looked over and watched as Brent approached, his chest out and an authoritative frown donned his brow. This did not bode well. Perhaps it was time to leave for the day. Athrin stood, packing his bag.

'I knew you'd be here,' Brent spat.

It was enough to give him pause, if for but a moment. 'This is my desk.'

'Not for long, funny man.'

Athrin threw his bag over his shoulder and turned to face him, now curious.

'I have received enough complaints about you,' Brent continued. 'You come in late, you harass the staff, and you berate your superiors.'

There was that twitch again.

Brent took a second to make sure enough eyes were on him to give him courage, then he turned to Athrin with a smile. 'You're fired.'

Athrin eyed him, this little man, with his quaffed hair and expensive suit. He wouldn't always have tolerated this. It was not lost on him; he was well aware of this man's intentions. But he promised.

'Don't bother begging. It's a done deal,' Brent continued, looking around for admiration and support. He clearly enjoyed this. But his smile and his pride burned away in an instant as Athrin took a step closer and stood in front of him. Turned out, he was a full head taller than Brent and held no malice towards him, no anger, perhaps only frustration. Brent's bottom lip may have been quivering under the weight of it, those dull, almost lifeless eyes and that featureless expression. It unsettled him for reasons he could not explain.

'Was there a problem with my work?' Athrin asked simply. He wanted to know this.

The groomed peacock struggled to find words. He stammered and was forced to take a step back before he could reassert himself. 'I don't know. But that's beside the point!' He summoned what he had left with renewed vigour. 'You –'

But before he could continue, Athrin walked off, leaving him to rant and rave all he wanted.

Athrin made his way to the elevator and tapped the button twice, watching the number as it counted up.

'How dare you walk away from me?' Brent roared and was heard before he was seen. He pranced around the corner and stood a good, safe, distance away from Athrin. 'I'm not finished with you.'

The numbers counted higher, almost there. Perhaps he should grab a pizza tonight, Athrin thought.

'Are you listening to me?!'

The loud ding, the doors opened and Athrin wasted no time. But as the doors closed a meticulous manicure held them ajar, barely.

'You have paperwork to sign and need to give a handover before you can go!' Brent stammered.

'I will tell you this, not because you deserve it, but because it was once my duty,' Athrin began, looking down at him. 'You should avoid Catherine.'

Brent gasped. The sound was comparable to that of a drowning man, as was the sight. 'How dare you!'

Athrin nudged him away with his foot and the doors closed. That was the last time he would ever see this floor.

*

The sun had set. The stars hidden behind thick clouds, and then the rain started.

Athrin stood in front of the diner. A very prominent 'closed' sign stared back at him. He would go hungry for a while longer.

In the rain he walked. His jacket took most of it but he did little to avoid getting soaked. He did not care.

No one was around, all had scattered and fled. Not a single dog bark, nor was there a stray cat, a cyclist or even a beggar. Everyone had a place to be.

He walked slowly. It gave him time to think and contemplate, figure out what he did wrong so that he could learn from it and avoid it next time. But he was unable to understand it, unable to pin one thing. Just like last time, or the time before that. The thought teased at his mind, like a buzzing fly, that maybe he was not meant for this life. Normal. It was such an ugly word.

It had been a long road. He wasn't ready to give it up just yet; it would not be right to break a promise.

He turned the corner, the rain still beating down upon him as if trying to drive him into the ground, but he was nearly there, nearly home. But then, he stopped.

Just ahead, at the base of the stairs and right in his path, was a girl. Long blonde hair clung tightly to her clothing from the rain. Even if it was only her profile, he could tell she was beautiful and a foreigner perhaps. She had not seen him yet. Her gaze fixed upon the stairs.

Once he had gathered himself, he approached. He needed to get past her.

When he was but a few feet away her head whipped in his direction, hair flailing wildly, her eyes like piercing gemstones as they latched onto his with a look of surprise. He did not know her.

The rain beating on the rooftops was almost deafening, but he could hear her clearly. 'I found you,' she said with a smile.

Before he could do anything, she locked him into an embrace, pulling him down a foot to wrap her arms around his neck. She kissed him.

The sound of the rain echoed around him. It pounded against the clay roof tiles, pooled into the gutters, flowed down the street and road, and gushed down the drains.

When Athrin's senses returned, he wrenched himself from her grasp, though she was still wrapped around his shoulders and offered only a smile. 'A few things...' he began.

But then her smile widened and she interrupted him with a sweetened giggle. 'You can die now.'

He could not see it. It was far too quick and far too sudden. She had pulled a weapon out of nowhere and slashed at him. Blood sprayed the ground.

Trails of crimson ran with the rain. It painted the concrete and the dirt, only to be washed away like it never was.

Chapter III

Blood And Water

Silence. For what felt like an eternity. He could feel nothing and sense nothing. But he knew he was alive; it would never be that easy. Death was not allowed.

'Athrin,' the voice whispered.

He tried to move but there was no response from his body.

'Athrin.' The voice grew a little more desperate, as if concerned.

He writhed wildly, seeking to answer the call. He could never and would never be able to deny her call.

'Get up!'

*

Athrin could feel his senses slowly creep back into his body. He could feel the cold of his clothes against his skin from the rain which still beat down on his back. It did not take long for a sharp pain to course throughout his body, radiating from the crown of his head to the tips of his toes, a reminder of what had brought him here to the precipice.

Fighting through the pain, which sought to overwhelm him, Athrin forced his body to move, wrenching himself from the ground and to a knee. It was all he could muster for now, struggling through the haze as his consciousness threatened to fade out at any moment. He found the source of the pain, a deep wound across his chest, which still oozed a steady stream of blood with every movement. His retired reflexes had barely saved him from a fatal wound.

There was a sound, sudden and quick. His body moved on its own, old instincts awakened from shock, and he managed to dodge the incoming blow, leaping away from the attack. Athrin leaned against the wall of the apartment building, applying pressure to the wound in hope of delaying as much blood loss as possible, then he turned to his assailant.

The woman stood a few feet from him, seemingly unperturbed by the rain as she stood there and stared at him. Crystal blue eyes glittering in the dim light, filled with what he could only describe as predatory curiosity, as a cat would observe a trapped mouse. 'Hmm… you should have played dead for a little longer.'

'Who are you?'

'That won't matter, you'll be dead soon.' Her words were a peculiar contrast to her sweet smile and voice.

'I would rather we not do this,' Athrin said carefully, buying enough time to staunch the bleeding and secure his footing.

'You're welcome to roll over and let me kill you without a struggle.' As she spoke, she whipped her weapon out to her side, announcing her intention and allowing Athrin to see it for the first time.

It was a sword. Difficult to make out in the dark as the blade melded almost completely with the night, but he could judge the length of it and prepare. Athrin watched her hand, read her posture. It was clear she knew how to wield it, but it would place her just above an amateur. Sloppy. He had been wounded by this person, the like of which would never have happened before. But, that was a long time ago. 'What do you want?'

'To kill you.'

He didn't recognise her, by appearance or reputation. She couldn't have been from the old days; she was someone new.

'Why?'

'Because…' She took a step forward. It seemed her patience had run out. 'You're the Dragon.'

The blade cut through the rain as she swung at him, with enough strength and skill behind it to kill almost anyone. But Athrin was cold, tired and sore. He'd not humour this any longer.

Her sword had stopped just shy of Athrin's neck. He had grabbed the blade with his bare hand and held it fast. She stared at his hand, noticing a thin trail of blood squeeze out and run down the length of the blade. Then she looked at him and caught his eye, rendered speechless. A cold, emotionless glare looked back at her, lifeless and devoid of any semblance of humanity. She had never seen such eyes.

'I am not who you are looking for,' Athrin said calmly, his tone the same as always, if a little quieter. 'You should look elsewhere.'

She tugged once on the sword, testing if she could wrench it free from his grip. She could not. 'Sounds like something the Dragon would say.'

'I knew the one you are looking for, but they are no longer in the city.'

'That's convenient.'

Athrin pulled on the sword, bringing her a little closer and her eyes back to his. 'I do not want to fight,' he said clearly, tempering his tone as best he could. 'But if I must, I will.'

'It's you…'

'It is not.'

Athrin released the blade as she tugged on it again, separating them by a few feet. Still, she watched him, a semblance of doubt glittering in those wide blue eyes.

A moment later, she turned away with a firm 'hmph' and tossed her sword aside, which disappeared into thin air before reaching the ground. 'I'll be back for you.'

*

He stumbled into his home, dropping his bag and ignoring it as the contents spilled and rolled across the floor. He clawed his way from wall to wall until he reached the bathroom, a trail of blood dotted between each muddy footprint. He threw open the cupboard below the sink and pulled an aged medic pack from the back.

Through the fight he had fought this pain. As was his training. But he was fading, the blood he had lost and the blow he had sustained had brought him to an edge he had not felt in a long time.

The bandage around his chest was already soaked in blood. He administered alcohol and a special paste to the wound, inducing more pain, but then he wrapped a final bandage and allowed himself to slip to the ground and leaned against the wall.

He stared at the ceiling.

With a flick, he lit a cigarette and watched as the first puff of smoke swirled around the light.

He stared into the dull light.

After a while, he found himself smiling. Today was quite the day. And after all of that, he had slipped into his old world and suffered a glimpse of what he had left behind. He did not miss it.

His hand was shaking. He had not realised it until now. Slowly he raised it to the light and watched it, trying to figure out what was causing it. And then he knew. It got a chuckle out of him.

Adrenaline such like he had not felt coursing through his veins in a long time. The excitement. The rush. A very small part of him may have missed it.

*

The pounding rain continued. It was unrelenting and remorseless.

Athrin had spent a lot of time moving slowly from room to room. He had finished cleaning the floor of mud and blood as well as leaving the clothes he could salvage to soak. He doubted it, but perhaps they could be recovered.

He rubbed out an eighth cigarette amongst the others in the ashtray and watched the rain dance on the rooftops. It had been hours since he had bandaged his wounds for the second time. It was still difficult to move but the recovery was progressing well. Quick as always, aided by the salves he had kept from the old days.

When he had seen enough of the rain, he returned to the apartment. Still no lights on inside. He slowly wandered from wall to wall, checking the floor for any spots he might have missed. Eventually, he found himself standing in front of a closed door to one of the rooms, a bedroom. He stood in front of it and placed his hand upon the wood. He dared not enter. He just stood there.

After a while, he tore himself from the thoughts and the memories and moved sluggishly towards the couch. There he collapsed onto the sheets and buried his face in the pillow. This day was finally over.

Chapter IV

The Broken Tile

Almost a week had passed. Slowly and methodically, he packed his bag, planning out his trip with each item and its purpose. He would not go far, to the city and back, but he always did this.

As he left the apartment and locked the door, he noticed the wet grass and the light mist in the air. It was still early morning, but it seemed the rainy season was not over yet. He did not necessarily like the rain but was glad to see it stay for a while longer.

Once at the bottom of the stairs, he noticed the dark patch on the ground. He had done his best to clean what the rain did not wash away, and no one would notice it if they did not know what had transpired. It did not give him pause but was a good reminder. Perhaps his time in this place was at an end.

The walk was long and uneventful. A school kid here, an office worker there, the few people about were the early birds, the ones he imagined himself to be. Mental notes.

He stood on the station platform, three minutes to go, and took a look around for the first time. A dozen people here, some on this side and a few on the other. But in the corner of his eye, one of the featureless goers caught his attention. They were unlike the rest. He recognised her instantly. The girl with the sword. He did not have time to fully identify her as the train arrived and separated them but he was fairly certain it was her. Perhaps she was following him.

From the train window he could no longer see her on the other side. Whether she had noticed or had moved on it did not matter, he would go about his business.

*

'So,' the woman began. Her suit was well tailored and her glasses sat neatly at the end of her nose as she glossed over the pages in front of her. 'Athrin? Am I saying that right?' She did not wait for a response. Her eyes met his and she was visibly taken aback. 'W-what makes you think you would be a good fit for our team?'

No one else was in this small meeting room. The small round table between them seemed insurmountable with the distance she sat away from him. 'Well,' he began, positioning himself neatly. 'I believe myself diligent. I keep to myself and perform what tasks I am given.'

'I see.' She pursed her lips, flipping one of the pages. 'From what I can gather you have been in the work force for only a few years. May I inquire what you did before?'

Some things came to mind. 'I travelled a lot,' he began. 'Once I returned to Seceena, I decided to settle down.' He got this question often; he had been told to answer it as such.

'I see.' Another flipped page, then another before she snapped the booklet closed and turned to him. 'Unfortunately, I do not think you'd be a good fit for us.'

He had expected as much. 'To better my future endeavours, may I ask why?'

'I don't think you'd work well with others.'

*

Athrin walked the city. Weaving between the crowds as they blindly marched from calendar entry one to two. Narrowly avoiding a woman with a pram, he watched as she continued on without even realising the concussion she had narrowly avoided. How she had survived this long was a mystery, he thought.

With another near miss here and another there, he reached the train station and this time he could not see any would-be aggressors, specifically ones wielding a sword, but he had a feeling they were somewhere.

*

'Athrin,' the chubby man said loudly, swaying back and forth in his chair as if he needed to be somewhere quite urgently. 'Can I call you Athrin?' He did not wait for a response. 'Have you been working in the industry long?'

It was a conscious effort to keep his expression neutral; he was finding anything short of standard was counting against him. 'For some time already, yes.' He sat neatly, his arms folded smartly on the table in front of him. 'I am familiar with multiple different systems and am told I pick up new things quite quickly.'

'Excellent!' the man exclaimed, bordering on yelling, and the swaying continued. 'Unfortunately, I don't think you're what we're looking for.'

He could feel the twitch. 'To better my future endeavours, may I ask why?'

'I think you're a little overqualified for this role.'

*

With a kick, the shoe flipped off his foot and joined its brother. He tossed the bag into the corner where it belonged and stood out on the balcony. The rain had stopped, but the water ran down the tiles and into the gutters. It poured over the streets and circled the drains.

He lit a cigarette and tossed the lighter aside. A puff of smoke hovered before him, dissipating slowly while it swirled and grew.

Athrin tapped the railing with his fingers, but not to a tune or a beat as he watched the flowing water.

'That's a dirty habit,' he imagined someone saying. He looked to his side, almost able to make out the imaginary person. 'What will you do now?' they may have asked.

'Nothing specific,' he might have answered, still watching the trickling streams. 'I will do what I can.'

He reached over, shooing the spectre as if it were a puff of smoke itself. Tonight, he did not want to remember; he did not want the memories creeping in. It was an uncertain time.

*

There was a pounding on the door. It caused Athrin to wake from the paper-thin veil of slumber he had achieved only a few hours ago. A window check confirmed it was morning, early, with the sun still barely peeking over the city.

The knocking continued.

Slowly, he wrenched himself from the sofa and the warmth, making his way towards the door. He wasn't expecting anyone. He had not ordered anything nor did he invite anyone.

He grabbed a jacket from the rack and pulled his arms through, then opened the door.

The girl that attacked him stood there, looking up at him, pouting. 'You took your sweet time. It's freezing out here.'

Cautiously he eyed her. She was not wielding her weapon and her stance was not adversarial but he had more than enough reason to suspect her.

'Can I help you?'

'Yeah…' She nudged him, perhaps to move past him inside, but he did not relent. 'You can let a girl in from the cold.'

He leaned out, checking around if anyone was with her, or perhaps if he could spot a film crew with accompanying 'pranked' sign. 'I would rather you killed me out here… just cleaned the carpet.'

She pushed him a little harder this time. 'Move, yo.'

'Yo?'

With the next shove he had almost fallen over, giving her a gap to slip through and enter his apartment. He didn't stop her, but this did not bode well, a possible – if not proven – enemy was in his home. He closed the door and followed her, knowing he may need to throw her out.

She was already in the kitchen, filling the kettle with water before slamming it to the base and switching it on. Afterwards, she promptly began searching the cupboards.

'Not here to kill me today?' he asked cautiously, giving her a wide berth.

'Not yet,' she said quickly, starting on the second cupboard. 'We'll see once the weather clears.' She paused, shooting him a look cold enough to challenge the weather. 'Mugs?'

'Sink, top left.'

A warmer smile and a robust twirl, she slipped to the mentioned cupboard and opened it, several generic dull cups packed neatly from left to right, but at the end of the row were two mugs which stood out: one green, the other pink. She turned to him again, this time with one judgemental eyebrow raised. 'The pink one yours?'

He did not respond. His eyes fixed on the mug in question, thoughts afire, the present dulled.

She took the pink mug and he may have pictured someone else in her place as she put it beside the kettle and looked around before locked eyes with him again. 'Where's the tea?'

His eyes refocused; the woman in front of him was not the owner of that mug. He snatched it from the counter so quickly and fiercely it was as if the mug was about to catch on fire. He replaced it and got her another mug from the row of greys, together with a box of teabags, and put it beside her.

All the while she was watching him, a mischievous smirk on her face. 'Mmhm… that was interesting.'

'Leave it.'

'Mmmm.' She popped the box and took a teabag, preparing the water and stirring lightly, her eyes still on him.

'Why are you here?'

She sipped the tea, flinching off the heat. 'Any milk?'

He answered with a glare, which did not go unnoticed, but was ignored.

She stirred in the milk, kicking the fridge closed, and returned her attention in his vague direction. 'Got any breakfast?'

'Why are you here?'

She sipped the tea, leaning over the counter on her elbows and smiling at him. 'Eventually, to kill you. But first, observing.'

He had not reached the end of the fuse just yet, but his patience was wearing thin. 'Observing?'

She nodded playfully, taking another sip. 'I have other business in the city besides killing you, so until I'm sure I decided to observe.'

'I told you already, I am not the Dragon you are after.'

'You did say that, yes.' She paced around the room, rubbing the mug between her hands and blowing the steam from the top while she examined his home. 'But you're still the most likely candidate.'

'Look…' he began, moving to cut her off but she slipped past him without spilling a drop. 'The one you are after is—'

'Athrin,' she interrupted him, spinning on her heels to face him. 'That's the name you go by now, isn't it?' She hid behind the tea, winking at him playfully. 'You can't hide it. I know things.'

'Clearly…' He approached her slowly.

She did not run. He stood in front of her and looked down at her. She still kept her eyes locked to his.

'I am not sure what you think you know, neither do I care, but I am not who you are looking for.'

She chuckled, and had won the starting contest. 'Then you have nothing to worry about.' With another twirl she resumed her unguided, and unsolicited, tour. 'So, you live alone?'

Enough. The fuse had run out. He took the mug from her and grabbed a fistful of her jacket. With a tug, he dragged her to the door and nudged her outside. She looked back at him with a pout and a tinge of surprise, but before she could offer retort in words or actions, he slammed the door and turned both locks. He didn't even give her a second glance.

Her motives were unclear, her goal inconsistent and chaotic. None of the things he could afford now. Gone were the times where he'd be intrigued or combative; he did not care for her games.

*

He shook hands with the woman after the meeting. She smiled brightly at him over the rim of her spectacles. 'Thank you for coming in today.' She released his hand finally and began to collect her paperwork from the table. 'You've been shortlisted and we will be in touch.'

'Thank you.' He nodded. But there was more needed, some gesture that would be normal in these circumstances. He offered a smile. Or at least he hoped that's what it was.

Luckily, she did not react. Success. She left the room and allowed him to make for the elevator to quickly see himself from the building. If he stayed too long something might go wrong, that's how it always felt.

Once on the street, he had the opportunity to take a deep breath. It had been a busy morning and he was glad to see the end of it.

The people around him hurriedly trotted from A to B; none of them seemed aware of each other, all of them in their own little world. Athrin threaded himself through them as he made his way towards the station. This building was not too far from transport; it would be good to work here. He needed to find a job soon. It had been more than a week already without. While he was not struggling financially, he was beginning to feel restless. He wanted to stay busy.

As he walked through the streets, something caught his eye. In the window of one of the many stores was a line of televisions, all of them duplicated with the news of the day, a large heading dictating the report: 'The President to visit Seceena.' He wasn't sure why this caught his attention; it was not something he took interest in but one of the news reporters was interviewing a person he thought he recognised. An older man, mighty in frame, short grey hair and a long scar over his left cheek. The man stood at attention as he answered the barrage of questions. Behind him stood several similarly grizzled men in tailored suits, possibly his bodyguards. Perhaps at one stage, this would have meant something to Athrin – this man's presence would have been relevant. But not anymore.

'The Order, again?' he heard a passer-by ask.

'Seems so,' his friend replied, sipping from a paper cup. 'They've been policing the city for over a year now.'

Not anymore. It didn't matter, it had nothing to do with him. Athrin steered himself towards the station, ready to bring an end to this day.

*

The tap ran, water circling the drain speckled with bubbles and soap. Athrin washed the cup by hand, slowly and methodically, keeping his mind empty.

It was late afternoon, an orange glow over the city and the rooftops, the people outside quietening down for the day, slowly but surely bringing their day to an end as well.

Athrin wandered around the apartment, finding something here and there to clean or pack away, but the place was already well-kept. He had a lot of free time on hand these days. He wanted to keep busy.

And now here he stood, again, the door to the closed-off room. He had not been in there for a while; maybe it needed a cleaning pass, he thought. His hand slowly made its way to the doorknob. He grasped it tightly, too tightly. He turned it and began to open the door. From the open crack, he could smell it. The familiar scent, it washed over him and surrounded his entire being. The door slammed closed. In the distance, a dog started barking. He let go of the doorknob. He could not go in.

Athrin sat on railing of the balcony, staring off into the distance, a waft of smoke trailing from the cigarette in his mouth. He fought to keep his mind blank. Thoughts and memories clawed at him as they tried to invade his sanity. But he resisted. Mostly.

A familiar warmth embraced him from behind, arms wrapped around his neck and a chin rested on his shoulder. He knew it wasn't real, one of those memories had breached his defences, but perhaps he had let it in.

'How was your day?' she may have asked once.

He grumbled. Ash fell from the cigarette to the street below.

'That good, huh?' Maybe she would have chuckled. 'Still working on your quest for civility?'

He did not respond. It was a ghost. A fragment of his memories he had buried. It was not real.

'You can do it, Athrin. I believe in you.'

The embrace tightened. Such warmth, such comfort, such tremendous peace. And in that moment, he wavered, his hand made to reach up and touch the arm embracing him.

But no one was there. It was a ghost after all. The chill returned, washed through him so suddenly and completely.

It was cold out tonight.

Chapter V

The Casting of Doubt

Hunger. The common ailment of the many. The quest of the few. And today's mission. Athrin closed the door behind him, tapped the front of his shoe on the floor to straighten it to his foot, then turned the key and locked the door.

When he turned to walk toward the stairs, someone was in his path. She looked at him with a frown.

'Aw, I was hoping to steal your breakfast.' She was not brandishing a blade this time either but still issued caution.

Athrin was hungry; this was becoming tedious. 'Do you always steal food from your victims?' He did not wait for an answer, instead squeezing past the deliberately small gap she left for him and continuing on.

'Most do not survive.' She followed him down the steps, skipping and dancing from side to side. 'And I'm doing you a favour.'

He shouldn't – it was pointless but he did. 'Oh?'

'What will happen to all your food when you're dead?' She caught up and walked beside him down the path. 'It's not good to waste.'

Just as he expected. Senseless. 'Still think I am your Dragon?'

'Still not sure.' She stretched her arms over her head with an accompanying groan. 'But you're still the most likely.'

Very few people were around, one here and one there; most people were at work or school. He wished to be one of them. 'Once upon a time the Dragon was my enemy, I fought it too. If you ask your contacts, I am sure they would confirm that.'

'Oh, so you were with the Order.'

He remained silent; he had already said too much.

'Not the Order then?' She examined his face. He ensured she would find no clues. 'The Girdan?'

He would not engage.

'Must be the Girdan, the Order doesn't have people like you anymore.'

She knew much it seemed. He had taken her for an outsider. Though she may still have been, he would resist the urge to ask; such matters were out of his hands now.

'You haven't asked for my name yet.' She drew a pout on her face. 'Quite rude honestly.'

That was not quite how he remembered it. 'Does it matter? Will I not be dead soon?'

He sensed it. A sword swung through the air; it stopped less than an inch from his neck. Perfect precision. She smiled at him from down the length of it. Then the dark blade vanished as she tossed it to the side. 'Sure,' she began. 'Lisara.'

He nodded slightly. 'Charmed.' Then walked on. As expected, she followed soon after.

'To be honest, I was not expecting you to be capable.' She caught up to him again, leaning a little forward to see his face. 'I was told you would be docile, but you could still hold your own.'

'The Girdan tell you that?' He could no longer resist the urge; perhaps it was a reactionary inquiry that had slipped past his walls.

'Maybe.' She smiled. The slip did not go unnoticed and she would press it. 'Are you curious?'

He fixed himself, readied the walls. 'Not at all.' Then abruptly turned into the diner, assuming she would not be able to follow him inside. He was wrong, of course.

He sat at a table and sure enough, she sat opposite him, resting her head on her hands, both elbows on the table. And proceeded to stare at him.

He resisted. An uncomfortable amount of time passed with them in silence. And with every passing moment her smile widened, she knew.

'What?' he caved finally.

'Nothing,' she said quickly. 'Why do you ask?'

Obviously, she was toying with him and seemed to take great pleasure in it. But he needed to know some things; he needed to get rid of her. 'You are staring.'

'Am I?' She tightened her glare at him. Then whipped around and called to the waitress, 'Excuse me, can you take our order please?'

'Our?'

The waitress approached, snapping gum as she formed some words. 'What can I get you, sweetie?'

'Coffee.' Lisara looked over to Athrin for a split second. 'Two.' Then she snatched the menu from his side of the table and ran a finger over the listings. 'And two breakfasts, please.'

A bubble of gum popped. The waitress had finished scratching in her notepad. 'Is that all?' she answered with a nod, though before leaving she leaned over to Athrin. 'Good to see you with another person, sweetie.' She winked. 'Got yourself a cutie.' Then walked off, leaving him with the aftermath.

Dreading the result, Athrin turned to Lisara. And of course, she had an extra-large grin across her face. 'Ooooo, we're a couple now.'

He grumbled a response; it was not worth correcting anyone and there was no need. He did not care what people thought and it would not be a problem for long.

'Nice place.' She looked around the establishment, not spotting anything of particular note. 'Nice food here?'

'Why are you following me?'

'Come on, Athrin. I told you why already.'

'No.' When her eyes finally ended on him again, she noticed the intent behind them. He seemed angry. 'Why are you following me?'

Her fingers played with the salt dispenser. It was clear she was suddenly uncomfortable. 'I came to the city to kill the Dragon.' She did not look at him. 'I don't have any other business.' Now she connected to his eyes again, like brilliant gemstones glittering in the light. 'You were my only lead. I have nowhere else to go until I finish my task.'

This he was not expecting. For one, it was the first earnest answer he had gotten from her; for another, he had not even considered it. Of course he didn't; his default was to ignore others, to feel nothing. But he had changed, or at the very least he wanted to believe that he had. Everything inside of his head was telling him to stop there and accept her answer. But there was another littler voice, the quiet one that was not his own, and that voice he could never ignore. So, he asked her, 'Are you alone in the city?'

She smiled again, quite differently from before, a little weaker or gentler. The sarcasm and attitude gone, if for but a moment.

The waitress returned. She delivered their coffee cups and hurried off again, the sounds of snapping gum accompanying her.

Lisara took the cup and sipped from it. 'You sure know how to treat a lady, huh?'

'You stabbed me first, if you remember.'

That smile remained.

'Sorry,' he mumbled, and to her surprise, he said, 'I did not mean to pry.'

Now she chuckled, amused by his sudden shift. 'You want to tell me about that pink mug?'

The table shook. Athrin had inadvertently kicked the table. He looked away quickly. 'Point taken.'

'So,' she began, stifling a giggle. 'What do you do?'

He was unsure how to answer this question; in his mind, she already knew. 'In what way?'

'In general,' she explained, gesturing out the window with a wave. 'I've seen you in the city some days; others you're just walking around the streets.'

Well, he had that confirmed – she was following him. 'Looking for work, been going to interviews.'

Now stunned, she stared at him, almost gaping. What he said seemed so odd to her, she must have heard wrong. 'Work... as in contracts or something?'

'No,' he responded simply, seeing, however, that it needed some elaboration. 'Office work. Data entry, mostly.'

'Wait...' She slammed her cup to the table, needing a moment to compose herself. 'As in, white-collar citizen work?'

Now he answered with but a simple nod.

She seemed perplexed, unable to formulate a proper response or a question. She settled for a simple, 'Why?'

'I was fired from my last job.'

'Okay... but why?!' She glared at him but his reaction was the same. He did not find it as odd as she did. 'You are obviously from some organisation. You have some skill but you choose citizen work!'

There were some points in there that he could have taken offense to; instead, he nodded again. 'Correct.'

'Why?!'

'I left that behind.' He gulped half his coffee down. It was getting cold. 'I am not a part of it anymore.'

Silence loomed for a time, enough of a gap for the waitress to bring out their food and refill their coffees. And still Lisara stared at him. She seemed beyond words. Almost.

'I suppose that explains why you didn't fight back.' Angrily, she poked the egg on her plate with a fork. 'Of all the people to send me after, how troublesome.'

Athrin took his utensils and carved the food on his plate. 'Does that mean I am off of your suspect list?'

'No!' She pointed a slice of toast at him. 'Just moved you nearer to the bottom.'

That was good. Perhaps. 'How long is this list?'

'One.'

'Page?'

'Name.'

Well, it's the thought that counts. The more he spoke with her and learned of her goal, the more he wondered from where she had come. She was woefully unprepared, especially considering the enemy she was hunting. If she was to be believed, the fabled Dragon, the immortal creature which ushered in war and strife wherever it went, hiding in plain sight amongst people. He knew a little about it; he had even seen it once, a long time ago.

He looked over to her, her full attention on her food. It was perhaps a while since she last ate a decent meal, he thought. This woman was a mystery and she was obviously trouble. The further he could distance himself from her, the better.

'What is wrong with you…' she mumbled, her attention had shifted back to him and his plate.

He did not respond, a forkful in his mouth and no clue as to what she was referring.

'You look as if you've been measuring your food with a protractor.' He had cut his food in perfect squares, everything segregated and stacked neatly.

With a shrug, he carried on. 'Your plate looks like two cats had a fight on it.'

For a while she glared at him, with a pout and her cheeks inflated; clearly, she wanted to say something but for whatever reason chose not to.

'Are you liaising with anyone in the city?' he asked, though unsure why. He wanted to distance himself from the issue, but perhaps pointing her in the right direction would be a step towards accomplishing that.

'Nope.'

A simple response, no doubt to allow her to eat quicker, but still enough. 'Perhaps you should.'

'Like whom?' A bread crust slid his way but was quickly recovered. He'd have to watch his fingers.

'Are you from a branch of the Order?'

'Nope.'

'Any other affiliations?'

'Nope.'

He sighed. She was beyond unprepared. He wondered if she truly had a mission here or was merely some sort of insane hermit. 'I know someone you can see. Perhaps they will have more information for you.'

'Oh.' She pushed her empty plate aside – it was spotless – and sipped from her cup as she peered at him over the rim. 'Someone from the good old days?'

That familiar twitch was forming again. 'Would that help?'

She smiled playfully, toying with her hair in a free hand. 'Maybe.'

'Good. It is on the corner of Birch Street. Stand there with your sword in hand and they will find you.'

She gasped. 'Athrin! That's no way to talk about a lady!'

He ignored her, finishing his meal and turning to the last of his coffee. 'Well, good luck.'

'I have no idea where that is, or even where we are for that matter.'

It was his turn for stunned silence. The waitress returned and took their plates, balancing them on one arm as she addressed them. 'Is that all for you two?'

Lisara turned to her with a bright smile. 'Yes, thank you so much!' She put her hands together and tilted her head to the side in thanks. 'It was absolutely divine.'

'That's good, sweetie,' the woman barked, bearing fangs in a manner that could faintly be identified as a smile. 'Here's the bill.' She smacked a strip of paper on the counter and left.

Lisara looked at the paper then slowly at Athrin, and that grin formed again. 'Would you get this one, honey-bear?'

*

'So, where are we going again?'

Athrin turned a corner, taking a moment to check the street name and confirm they were going the right way. 'To meet the contact I told you about.'

'Who are they?' Lisara followed close behind him, admiring the city as they walked about. It was clear she was not paying attention to him as she had asked many times during the relatively short trip.

'I will let them explain.' He turned another corner and quickly slid down an alleyway. He recognised this area. Even though he had not been here in quite some time, it still looked very much the same. 'But they share your goal and should be willing to assist you.'

'Should?' She leaned forward to make sure he saw her raised eyebrow.

'I will not speak for him. We can hear what he has to say.'

'Very diplomatic, Athrin, is your white collar showing?' She slipped past him and trotted down the alley; perhaps something caught her eye or more likely, her boredom had peaked.

This was the place. Athrin stood at the corner, a junction of alleyways. Dustbins lined the walls, stray trash bags between them, with the odd cat or rat here and there scurrying away at the sight of people. It was definitely a place no one would normally tread.

Lisara was nowhere to be seen, but he was sure she would not have gone far. This was his chance to be rid of the problem, help her find her way and keep her from interfering with him further. Truthfully, he did not want to be here. It was a line too close to returning to this life he had left behind, but he would not stay long. After this he'd have done enough for her, from here on it would be up to her. Even this was overstepping what he would normally do for someone. But he had his reasons.

'Well, isn't this a surprise.' A voice came from the dark. The man revealed himself and stood a few feet from Athrin. 'I didn't know what to think when you called.'

The man was as tall as Athrin, young but grizzled – it would be easy to mistake him for some street riffraff or thug if not for his friendly smile.

'Calem,' Athrin greeted and they shook hands.

'Good to see you, Athrin. It's been years.' He looked up and down the alleys, making sure they were alone. 'I heard about what happened. My condolences.'

'Thank you.' Athrin remained expressionless.

'So, to what do I owe the honour?' He smiled. 'Are you working again?'

'No.' Athrin intended to correct such assumptions quickly. 'I would rather not stay long. I brought someone to see you.'

'Oh?' He was intrigued now, checking the alleys again before he continued. 'You did mention that. Where are they?'

'Behind you.'

Calem jumped forward suddenly. Obviously, he had not sensed her presence until now. Lisara stood where he was, her hands behind her back and a mischievous smile on her face.

'Greetings.'

'Calem, Lisara. She is hunting something in the city and has no contacts here. It should be of interest to you as well.' Athrin took a step closer to her. In the event she did something out of the ordinary, he wanted to be ready to stop her.

Calem eyed her cautiously, still a little startled. 'We are not fond of outsiders, Athrin. They complicate things.'

'Preaching to the choir.' Athrin dodged a kick to his shin. 'Lisara is hunting the Dragon.'

All caution was quickly replaced by shock. Calem gawked at Athrin then back to Lisara. 'The Dragon? You can't be serious.' He waited a moment, hoping someone would tell him it was a joke. No one did. 'It's in the city?! You're sure?'

She pointed to Athrin. 'It's right here.'

Quickly shooing her hand, Athrin interjected, 'She suspected me at first, hence why I came to you.'

'I see...' Calem examined Lisara, probably coming to a similar conclusion as Athrin. 'Well, it's our duty to be prepared for it, so naturally we would welcome your help.' He looked at Athrin again. 'Provided she's not delusional.'

'You know, I'm right here.'

'She may be delusional, but I believe she is telling the truth.' He turned to Lisara and motioned towards her hand.

She rolled her eyes, but responded. With a flick of her wrist, she pulled a sword out of thin air and held it in front of her, allowing a moment for the realisation to set in, and then tossed it to the side as it disappeared.

'A Blade Bearer!' Calem exclaimed, excited by the prospect as all doubts seemed to melt away. 'There are so few left. Which school do you come from?'

'I don't want to tell you.'

There was an awkward but brief pause. 'Fair enough.' He looked around again, still wary of spying eyes. 'Come, let's get off the street.'

Athrin had now completed his task; it was time to leave. He turned to walk away. 'I will leave it to you.'

Though Calem quickly stopped him. 'Athrin, please, let me at least treat you to a cup of coffee for coming all this way.'

There were many reasons to turn down this offer, very few, if any, to accept it. But when Athrin looked at Lisara, he could not help but worry; perhaps not for her safety, but for anyone inside. Nevertheless, against his better judgement, he followed.

*

The hall was wide and stretched far. The dim lights did nothing for the heavy shadows and darkened corners, but lit enough to make out the various posters and scribbled maps that could be seen lining the walls. Some of the rooms on either side no longer had a door and groups of people could be seen chatting, eating, or sleeping within. At one stage this building might have been an extravagant hotel, but now it was a den for miscreants and exiles.

'So who are you?' Lisara asked, twirling around as she took in the surroundings, her hands behind her back.

'We're a group of outcasts. In our own way we keep the city safe from the shadows and sometimes from the Order.' Calem guided them down another hall. 'We take in the defectors from the Order, and any of those willing to help fight.'

'So you're the Girdan?' she asked, pausing in front of an open door, where inside was what looked like holding cells, a few guards keeping watch over what seemed like empty cells.

'At one stage we might have been called that.' Calem stopped and turned to them. 'But that name has been tarnished as of late.'

Lisara spotted someone in a cell, perhaps the only person here. It looked to be a woman huddled in the corner, muttering to herself and seemingly deprived of sanity, untouched food beside her. 'Who is that?' Lisara asked Calem, who turned to leave and continued guiding them.

'The one who tarnished it.'

Athrin walked by the holding cells, taking a single glance inside at the woman before following them.

'Here.' Calem served them both a cup of coffee then sat with them, holding his own. 'So, Athrin, how did you two come across each other. You couldn't have been working?'

Truth be told, Athrin was hesitant to retell the story. He would prefer it faded into the deep, dark recesses of the sea. Unfortunately, it was not up to him.

'I stabbed him,' Lisara said quickly, casually. She sipped her coffee and looked around the room for something to pique her interest.

Calem looked to Athrin for confirmation. His silence was enough. 'Why?!'

'I was sure he was the Dragon,' she replied simply. 'Funny story, really.'

Athrin said nothing, rolling his eyes away from them. He spotted something against the wall. A board of pictures and documents all connected by an intricate web of coloured string, and at the centre was a blurred photo of a man with a scar on his cheek. Out of habit, his mind immediately connected the dots and drew parallels. This was the plan for something. Something he would now ignore.

'What group are you from?!' Calem exclaimed. Their conversation had continued without him; no doubt he was running through the same questions Athrin had asked and no doubt becoming just as frustrated.

'I don't want to tell you.'

'Fine!' he yelled, sipping his coffee. It had a calming effect. 'I'll get some people on the street asking questions – if that fails, we'll risk a trip to the Oracle.'

'I will remain on standby until then.' She sipped slowly, then let out a deep sigh. 'Such hard work.'

With a grumble Calem now turned to Athrin, who was a little happier now that she wasn't his problem. 'What will you do, Athrin?'

'Nothing,' he replied simply. 'This is not my business anymore. I will leave her with you.'

'Hmm.' Calem sighed sadly. 'I thought you came to join us for a moment there.' He met Athrin's eyes and held them. 'I won't lie, we need someone like you. We're on the losing side, Athrin.'

Athrin could not help him.

'Ever since the Order went out into the public, it's been harder for us to maintain any kind of stability. Given the incident a few years ago we were splintered as it was.'

Athrin would not help him.

'I know what you've been through, Athrin, but we can really use you. Even if you just think about it…'

'You… know?'

Silence fell amongst them. Even Lisara was taken aback. She had not heard this dark tone from Athrin before.

'How could you possibly know?'

Calem flinched as Athrin looked at him, that narrowed glare few would see, but it only lasted for a moment before Athrin looked away again.

'Athrin, I meant no harm—'

'Thank you for the coffee, Calem.' Athrin stood quickly and put the cup down beside Calem's. 'It was good to see you. I hope we do not meet again.' Then without waiting for any response, he left, leaving them in silence.

That silence lasted for a good while, long enough for Athrin to have left the building, but there was someone who could not stand it any longer.

'Wow!' Lisara exclaimed. 'That was bizarre. What did you do?!'

'Nothing!'

'That didn't seem like nothing.' She leaned closer to him. 'I thought he was going to stab you!'

'It felt like he was going to do a lot worse...'

'Well, nah, not Athrin.' She waved a hand in the direction of the hallway with an accompanying scoff. 'He's harmless.'

'Harmless?!'

'He didn't do anything to me, and I stabbed him!' she said so proudly, her nose in the air.

'How you are still alive, let alone here, is a miracle.'

'What's that supposed to mean?'

Calem leaned a little closer to her first, as he didn't want even the slight possibility that Athrin could overhear them. 'You really have no idea who he is, do you?'

Chapter VI

The Last Light

The clouds gathered. Ominous and vast, consuming and utterly overwhelming the sky and sunlight, the rolling of thunder and approaching lightning visible in the featureless swell. All wanderers, young and old, large and small, ran for cover. A storm was coming.

Athrin walked slowly, his path long and his time abundant. He had cleared his head with this walk home. Now all he had to do was keep it that way.

A single drop of rain fell to his shoulder. He felt the cold as it seeped into his clothing. He looked up, and then the rain started in earnest. He approached a sheltered bus stop and stood in its cover. With a quick glance over the nearby map, he found he was still a lengthy distance from home. Perhaps he would wait here for the weather to clear.

He took to the bench, admiring the dancing rain on the pavement and the road. He watched as the puddles turned to pools and ran toward the drains. He always did like the rain, at one stage, but not anymore. Now it was a reminder.

*

'I asked him,' Lisara began. 'He didn't answer, I assumed he was a soldier. Like you, I guess, just not as dirty.'

'Ha!' Calem laughed, either ignoring or mistaking the insult. 'He was in the Order a long time ago, but he left with a brother in arms and joined the Girdan of old. But he was no mere soldier.'

'Don't tell me… data entry?'

'What? No!' He waved angrily at her, hoping it would quiet her. It did not. 'At the time, the Order would have called him an equaliser.'

Lisara sat, leaning on her arms, her legs swaying back and forward under the table.

'They would send him to clean up,' he added.

'I see,' she mumbled, her focus still teetering perilously. 'With a mop?'

But he ignored her. Perhaps she didn't understand, so he would need to make it clearer. 'In the Girdan we had another name for him. A Blade Breaker.'

*

It had returned. The ghost from his mind, the fragment of his memories. It skipped from puddle to puddle and twirled in the rain. Every now and then it would call out to him, laughing happily, but he ignored it. He had to.

The rain pounded on the cover over him; he listened intently to its dulcet tone, anything to distract him.

'Athrin,' the voice called to him, so close as if standing right in front of him. He could have pictured it, had he wanted to.

'Do you know why I love the rain?' she might have asked.

He knew. Of course he knew.

'It's like the world's taking a shower, everything feels so clean and fresh.' Another twirl and a skip, then a sudden stop with a playful glance back at him, he could feel the weight of it. It shook him. 'And it would always bring you home.'

*

44

'Right. I know them, so?' Lisara muttered disinterestedly while rolling the cup along the table.

'Then you know he is incredibly dangerous.'

'He didn't seem so.'

Calem massaged his temples. 'You know what, never mind. I feel bad talking behind his back anyhow.' He stood and grabbed the cups from the table, robbing Lisara of her toy. 'Let's discuss your Dragon hunt.'

'Haven't we already?' With a dissatisfied groan, she sprawled herself across the table in protest.

'No.' He dumped the cups into the sink. 'Let's start with how you know the Dragon is here?'

'Because they told me it's here. They wouldn't send me out for nothing. Duh.' Her voice was muffled as she had smeared herself across the table and spoke into the wood.

'And who are "they"?'

In response she merely mumbled something that resembled, 'I don't want to tell you.'

'Then what do you want to tell me?'

'You suck and I'm bored!'

'Then go on rounds with a team!' He spun around to yell at her more directly, only to find she was not here anymore. Calem ran to the hallway, hoping to catch sight of her, but she was long gone already.

*

Athrin walked through the rain. It didn't matter anymore. Escape was what he needed now. Even though he knew he could not outrun this threat, he had to try. Still, he could hear the jovial laugh and the voice calling to him, but he ignored it. This would fade eventually, as it always did.

He needed to reroute his thoughts, any sort of distraction. Yes. That would do. One problem was out of his way now; he had done more than his share and delivered her to Calem – no doubt she would be able to accomplish her mission and even have a place to stay. Calem was desperate enough for people he would offer her anything to be able to add her to the ranks. And she'd take it. Probably.

Lightning and thunder flashed and echoed in the distance – a bad omen for some but a beautiful sight for others.

At a corner, he stopped, traffic blocking his way. He looked back and noticed the spectre had gone. This was good, he could have some peace for a while. Or so he thought.

Just as he turned a corner, his building in sight, something caught his eye. A feeling of déjà vu washed over him. Lisara was here, in front of his apartment building, soaking wet from the rain. She stared up at the sky, almost as if she could see more than the dark grey veil, and appeared completely unperturbed by the downpour. Begrudgingly he approached her and threw his jacket over her small frame. 'You will get sick if you keep doing this.'

She looked over to him, after a moment, as though she had returned from some far-off place and only just noticed his presence. There was a strange tinge of sadness in her eyes, but she smiled at him all the same. 'Will you let me kill you now?'

Athrin led her towards the staircase and under cover from the rain. She offered little resistance. 'Are you going to kiss me again?'

With a quick movement she grabbed his shirt and threw him against the wall, then, with her hand still pinning him in place, she leaned in closer. 'Do you want me to?'

Athrin frowned at her, their eyes but a breath apart. This girl seemed to love toying with him. He could not understand why and he did not appreciate it. Those eyes. Like sapphires glittering in the dim light. They reminded him of her.

He pushed her away and climbed the stairs. He didn't care if she followed, but knew she would and even if he was angry, it was for the best. Leaving her out in the cold rain would weigh heavily on the conscience many told him he did not have.

He opened the door and let her in, quickly disappearing down the hall to grab two towels from the laundry. He returned and tossed one over her head and grabbed his jacket from her shoulders. Then he began to wipe his face. 'Shower is down the hall. You should use it.'

But she stood in place, right where he had left her, the towel still over her head. Rain fell from her hair to the floor, forming a puddle around her bare feet.

He noticed this and considered leaving her to whatever thoughts might be going through her head; instead, he leaned closer. 'Lisara, dry your hair at least.'

The towel swayed as she nodded. Her hands found the top and she wiped her hair, wandering her way blindly around the room. Athrin guided her down the hall to the bathroom and let her inside, closing the door behind her. 'Drop your clothes outside, if you want me to wash them.'

A mumbled response came from within.

He leaned against the wall, still drying his hair, and waited for her. The sound of the pounding rain and dull thunder outside intensified, drowning out anything else. He was glad to have made it back in time before the full force of the storm.

'Athrin.'

His hands stopped. It was difficult to hear her through the surrounding torrent, but he waited.

'You know why I came here, right?'

The back of his head touched the wall, he could imagine where this was going, and he wasn't ready for it just yet. 'To kill me, no doubt.'

The door opened slightly and clothes fell on the ground, accompanied by a curt remark. 'No doubt.' Then the door closed again and water began running from the shower.

Athrin bent over and grabbed the clothes, carefully, and while averting his eyes. Before walking away, he paused at the door again. To a certain extent, he thought he could understand what might be going through her head, for once upon a time he too was like a stranger in a strange city. He was fortunate that back then there was someone for him. Hopefully there would be someone for her.

*

The washing machine tumbled, the rain pounded, and the shower came to a stop.

Athrin stood out on the balcony. He watched the rain and tapped the half-length cigarette against the ashtray. He heard a rustle behind him.

'Glad the lightning is gone.' Lisara emerged. She stood next to him and looked out over the city.

He tapped the ashtray again. 'Scared of the lightning huh?' He looked over to her, expecting a snappy comeback. Instead, he noticed she was in clothes he recognised. Those pants and that sweater were not hers.

'Not scared,' she said quickly, almost defensively. 'I just don't like it.' Then she noticed his pause and knew what brought it on. 'The clothes you left were not my size.' She pulled on the sweater's shoulder and smoothed it over her figure. 'I found these in the laundry basket.'

He merely grumbled, looking back to the city and the rain. He tapped the cigarette to the ashtray again and decided to disregard it. They were only clothes.

'So,' she began, still staring at him, perhaps trying to catch his eye. 'You're not mad at me?'

Smoke trailed off from his breath. 'No.' He wasn't sure why she'd think him mad; the clothes or her return to his home were the two options he could think of. 'Why did you come back?'

It seemed he picked the correct option, as her mood shifted. 'I'm not sure. I didn't feel comfortable there.'

Yes, perhaps Calem scolded her when she tried to steal something or denied her free roam within his home. Perhaps he should do the same. Had he the heart.

'You will need Calem's help.' He tapped the ashtray. 'I cannot help you through the city.'

Lisara snatched the cigarette from his mouth. He watched her but did nothing. Slowly she put her lips to the end and drew from it, letting out a steady, long stream from pursed lips. After a moment had passed and the cloud dissipated, she offered it back to him, eyeing him curiously. Instead, and to her apparent disappointment, he took the stub and scrunched it in the ashtray.

'Apparently…' She leaned on the railing, still eyeing him. 'You're more than meets the eye.'

Vague. Too vague. 'Okay.' He rested his back on the rail, looking at the sky to watch the rain fall over the cityscape.

'You could search with me, clear your name, as it were.' She may have winked, but he wasn't looking at her.

'No.' His response was simple and firm. Helping her was one thing, but he would not let her pull him into that world again. He did not want to get involved. 'Calem will help you.' Now he looked at her, she was pouting, with puffed up cheeks. 'You should go back to him tomorrow.'

Lisara faked a gasp, clasping a hand over her mouth. 'Athrin! Does that mean you want me to stay the night?'

'Not at all,' he responded quickly and without pause. 'I would prefer you went back tonight.'

Another gasp, a little louder, and with a second hand to her mouth. 'That does hurt a little bit.'

'Stay here, go back, do whatever you want.' He hoisted himself from the rail and went inside. She remained for a moment before trotting after him.

With her hands clasped behind her back, she slowly walked around the room, examining everything again from top to bottom. 'So, which room can I use?'

'This one.' Athrin stood at the sink and turned on the kettle. 'There is only one bedroom, and it is… off limits.'

She turned to the couch and noticed the blankets on one of them. 'You sleep here?'

He nodded, adding sugar and coffee to an inch of milk in a mug.

'But there's a room.' She spun around and pointed to the door, as if spotting an endangered critter. 'Right there.'

He nodded again, stirring the contents while waiting for the water to boil. 'It is not my room.'

Her head tilted to one side, answered but puzzled. 'I see…' She shot him a sudden glare, as he was pouring boiling water into the mug. 'We're not going to sleep in the same room, are we…?'

He glanced at her out the corner of his eye as he stirred his mug. 'There are three couches. Take your pick. Or leave, same thing.'

'What if I stole the bed for an evening?' She tiptoed to the door. 'I'm sure whoever wouldn't mind, or even notice.' Her hand inched closer to the door.

'Lisara.' His tone was enough to stop her. He had not intended it to be as stern as it was, but it did stop her. 'Please, do not go in there.'

Her hand and her curiosity retreated. But the pout remained. Perhaps she did not want to push his good graces too far lest he throw her out.

With a mug in one hand, he tossed a blanket at her and took a seat on the other side of the table. 'Loo is down the hall. Nighty night.'

Lisara wrapped the blanket around herself and curled up on the couch. She smiled mischievously at him. 'You're a real charmer, Athrin.'

After taking a sip, he put the mug aside and fell to his back, waving a hand in the air toward her general direction. 'I try.'

*

It was dark. It was cold. It was quiet. He did not know this place; he had never been here before. This was a dream, there was no other explanation, yet he was cognisant and fully aware.

As he moved around this darkened area he could tell, with some certainty, that he was not alone. There was something here with him, something that knew exactly where he was. He could feel the gaze upon him.

In the dark there was movement, something akin to a slithering mass, accompanied by a dull, vibrating rumble. Yet he could not see anything.

And then, in the dark void before him, he could feel a tremendous presence draw nearer. Two glowing orbs appeared, attesting to the size of whatever this thing was, it glared at him, and a warm wind accosted him, accompanied by a horrible snarl. He could sense this beast thought of him as prey. It was as if it measured him, judged him.

After a time, it receded back into the darkness and the presence disappeared as if it had never been.

CHAPTER VII

DISPARITY IN THE MUNDANE

A rustle from within.

The rain had stopped sometime last night; now the dew sat on the grass and glistened in the sun as it peaked over the horizon and between the buildings. It was a fresh feeling this morning.

More rustling near him, louder and more intentional this time, it was enough to draw him from his abnormally deep sleep. He opened his eyes and immediately his blood ran cold. Lisara was laying with him, curled up and latching onto his side, an unmistakably wide grin on her face. She seemed asleep, squeezing him tighter.

He was surprised she managed this without waking him. He was normally a light sleeper. With a tug he tried to free his arm, but her grip tightened and she snuggled more fiercely.

Well, he did not want this to go on much longer. With a sigh and a quick, vicious tug he freed his arm and wrenched himself from her grasp. She slumped back into place, wriggling and squirming until she was comfortable again.

Athrin pulled his jacket on, grumbling and growling under his breath, disappointed that she was able to sneak up on him. Maybe he was losing his edge.

'You're no fun,' she teased.

He looked back at her for a moment then after a quick zip of his jacket, he went for the kitchen. 'Oh yes, how dare I.' He flicked on the kettle. 'Coffee?'

She rolled over and bunched up the blankets to huddle herself in a ball. 'That'd be delightful, dear butler, two sugars and a scone please.'

He almost chuckled. He grabbed two grey mugs from the cupboard and prepared them as the water boiled. Against his better judgement, he looked over to her. She was looking back at him, sort of. Huddled and warm, her eyes were partially open and with a satisfied smile on her face.

'You seem to have slept well.'

She nodded while maintaining the same expression. 'Hmm, yes. Nothing beats a bed and a warm body.'

'None of those things apply.' He stirred in the water, mixing quickly. Vigorously.

'Awww admit it, Athrin.' She waved at him through the blanket. It sank back slowly. 'We made it to second base.'

He stood in front of her, holding the two mugs of coffee. He was tempted. 'I have half a mind to pour this over you.' But it was his blanket, and his home, that he would need to clean.

When she realised he was there, she quickly unravelled her hands and snatched one mug from him, holding it close as if it was the only source of heat. 'Don't blame me if you cannot acknowledge this relationship.'

He sat on the other couch, far from her, opposite the table. 'You mean the relationship where you freeload and also stabbed me?'

'It was one time, Athrin!' She sipped the coffee, flinching from the heat and fanning her tongue. 'You don't have to keep bringing it up.'

He shrugged. 'One of us has to.'

She faked a gasp, nearly spilling her coffee. 'You acknowledge us!'

'No, not at all.' He corrected her quickly, avoiding a spill of his own. 'There is no "us", only you and your Dragon hunt, and me and my job hunt.'

With another sip she narrowed her eyes on him. Her gaze zipped between him and the door he had made clear was off limits. She drew a few conclusions in her mind. 'Bad relationship in the past?' She'd start with that one.

Athrin seemed to ignore her at first, taking a long time to drink, but then he responded, a little quieter than normal. 'I would rather not talk about it.'

She noticed the subtle change in his mood. He had gone from semi-casual and almost immediately transitioned down to what she viewed as 'normal' Athrin. 'So, a bad breakup huh?'

Now he would ignore her.

That grin returned. 'Nailed it,' she mumbled, dodging a glare from him.

Silence wafted between them for a time, broken up only by the intentional, gentle slurps from Lisara. She sighed loudly. 'So, Athrin the Blade Breaker, eh?'

He coughed. Some coffee may have been snorted, a minimal spill luckily. But there was a bigger issue than mere coffee stains. He snapped to her. She smiled normally as if she had said nothing overly surprising. He quickly drew a conclusion to where she would have heard that. Calem. 'A long time ago, I was called that.'

'I knew you weren't some white-collar Joe, but to think that you were a Breaker, that's kind of surprising.'

'I am not anymore. As I have said many times already; I left that world behind.' He finished off his coffee. 'No one believes it, but I am done.'

'That's the part I still don't get.' She put her empty mug on the table and then freed herself from the blanket cocoon so that she might interrogate him further. 'What made you abandon it?'

Athrin rolled the mug between his hands; he seemed deep in thought. It could be he did not know how to answer the question – it could have been he did not know if he should answer it at all – but after a time, he did. 'Because I was shown another way.' He returned to thought. Lisara admired the look on his face. 'And I no longer saw the point of it all.' His hands stopped; he may have lost himself for that moment but collected his thoughts quickly.

She let that linger, thinking on it and what he may have meant by it. But she could not figure it out; to her it did not make any sense. He had the skills and thus the responsibility. He should be obligated. Like she was. She lifted and tapped the mug on the table to catch his attention. It worked. 'If you have power, you owe it to the world to use it.'

He didn't necessarily think she was wrong, but how she said it did not sit right with him. 'Not if people will suffer because of it.'

'People?!' She threw her arms in the air. 'Most people don't even know what's happening around them. Why should you care about that?'

He put his mug on the table; he hadn't meant to but the slam echoed around the room. He looked at her without anger but something nearer to indifference. It was clear this discussion was not new for him, and this tired argument was wearing on him. 'If it cannot be used to help people, it should not be used at all.'

After a stunned pause, Lisara let out a sound that sounded like a cross between a sneeze and a scoff. She stared at him. 'What nonsense is that?!'

Athrin stood abruptly and snatched both mugs from the table. It was quite apparent that he wanted this conversation to be over.

'You're a Blade Breaker, Athrin. You can tear into people's minds. Those are not your words, and I doubt you believe them.'

He maintained his silence. Dropping the mugs into the sink, he started the tap and grabbed a sponge.

'Helping people is a waste of time. You can't help them all and few would thank you for it.' She stood angrily, facing him.

Slowly he soaped up the mugs, rinsing them thoroughly; afterwards, he put the sponge aside and turned the tap off. Then his hands remained still for a moment, as if considering something. 'Should I not help you?'

'That is different, Athrin,' she snapped. It was clear to her, the distinction between the people out there and the people in here. Could he not see it, or did he choose this ignorance? Either way she could not approve. 'We are hunting things the people out there don't even know exist. If we don't stand up to it and do whatever it takes, who will?'

'Your task, not mine.'

'And then what? You sit at an office desk and squander your abilities and power?' She took a step towards him, not to threaten him, but out of frustration, though he did not respond to it either way.

After a pause, in which time she was expecting an answer from him, Athrin left and disappeared down the hall. She watched him with a half gape.

'Don't ignore this, Athrin. It's irresponsible for you to be among these people.' She stomped her feet a few times until she was in front of the hallway. 'Why don't you understand?'

He emerged, a bundle of clothing in hand. '*You* do not understand.' He handed her the clothing he had freshly washed and tumbled – her clothing. 'Go after your Dragon, before it gets away.'

*

'Athrin, thank you for coming in today.' The woman shook his hand then quickly ushered him into one of the side rooms.

The room was small, a single round table and two chairs. It felt almost as if he had been in this same room each meeting, at each company, perhaps they all shopped at the same store.

The familiar woman sat opposite him and gestured for him to sit. He obliged, then she unpacked the folder she was carrying with her and spoke while her nose was buried in the notes. 'So this is round two, where I'll be asking you a few more questions.'

He nodded politely. At least he hoped he did.

'So, let's get right to it.' She looked up at him now, folding her arms neatly over the table. 'What made you decide to leave your last position?'

Death, despair, blood, the screams and probably the smell. But maybe she meant the other one. 'Management change and redundancies.'

'I see.' She ran a single nail across the edge of a page, then looked at him again. 'How would you deal with conflict in the work place?'

Blood splattered to the walls, the screams echoed through the basement. And other previous instances came to mind, none of them relevant to this particular conversation. 'If completely unavoidable; through conversation and understanding.'

'I see.' She flipped a few pages effortlessly and with a single motion of two fingers. 'When faced with a deadline, how do you react?'

It was a rainy night, the wind strong and the woods filled with people and things out to kill him, but he aimed and fired. Though, this was a little different. 'Remaining calm and collected. Recklessness will not solve the problem.'

'I see.' She flipped all the pages from one pile to the other with one fell swoop. Then she slid a pamphlet towards him. 'Nearly done, thank you. Just fill out this form and we can be finished.'

*

He had left the building. Returned to the city streets and walked among the people. He watched them pass him by, watched as they went about their business, fascinated with the autonomous nature of the people and how effortless they seemed to make it. Normal. It was something he tried to imitate. Not to fit in, not to find a place of belonging, he had that, but rather to not stand out. For a long time standing out got him in trouble, it risked the safety of those around him.

But... he was alone now. And suddenly the thought occurred to him: for whom was he pretending?

He collided with another person, a moment too late to dodge them, he had allowed himself to be caught unaware for that single breath. Unacceptable. He turned to the person to offer his apologies; she looked back at him. The spectre. The ghost. The one he lived for. She was right here, and smiled at him.

'Excuse me!' A shrill voice broke through the trance, bringing him back to reality. It was not a ghost but a rather disgruntled woman. It was not her. 'Don't just stand there like an idiot!'

Athrin forced himself to the present. He bent over and helped her collect the things that had spilled from her purse.

'Are you stupid?!' she cursed at him as she frantically collected her belongings. 'You should watch where you're going!' she continued to yell at him, snatching the things he had picked up for her. Once she had collected all the oddities and vague necessities, she turned to him and offered her full aggression. 'You should watch where you're going!' she repeated angrily.

He looked at her, still taken aback and surprised. He had other thoughts on his mind that weighed more heavily on him than this. 'Sorry.'

She stamped her foot in rage. 'You need to calm down!' she cried.

His attention returned to her for a moment, long enough to be slightly angered by the absurdity but not long enough to respond. He walked away from her, the screams and shouts faded into the distance behind him.

*

Athrin decided to take the train home today. It was always noisy and always busy; he hoped it would drown out his thoughts. He was wrong.

The ghost was here. In the reflection of the glass window, he could see her sitting on the railing, humming and swaying back and forth. Occasionally she would look in his direction. He watched her intently. Longingly.

'You know, don't you?' Her voice echoed in his ears, so familiar, and so very heavy.

The scenery outside whizzed by quickly, trees and buildings nothing but a blur. Vein-like trails of water pulled across the glass as the train cut through the rain. The occupants of this car were few, a cough here and a wheeze there, nothing overly obtuse.

'That's what you're worried about, right?' her voice asked gently.

He dared not look now.

The train left the city centre and the suburbs came within view. His stop was the second one. It could not come fast enough.

'Athrin.'

He looked.

'You have to let me go.'

'Calem.'

He turned to the voice, and cringed immediately when he saw who it was. 'Oh, you.'

Lisara stood in front of him, having quickly closed the gap from across the hall. 'You're such a charmer.'

Quickly he stuck a pose with his hand on his chin and a wink at an audience that wasn't there. 'It's a gift.'

She shoved him playfully, but with enough force to nearly knock him through the wall had he not stopped himself. He was clearly surprised by it.

'Your boy scouts find anything?' she asked quickly.

Needing a moment to centre himself, Calem then took to strolling down the hall. She followed. 'There is definitely something amiss in the city. And it's not the Order's movements spurring it.'

'And that translates to…?'

'Means: no.' He didn't look back and neither did he stop. 'But we'll keep looking, as I said, there is something different.'

'Boring.'

'Then why not do something?' He stopped now, having reached his destination, a table with a map and another man standing near it. 'There's a thing you can take care of.'

'A thing?' She stood beside him and peered at the map, her nose pulled up at the prospect of exerting effort.

With a quick nod he put a finger on the map. 'Here.' He motioned towards the man. 'Nandla found something.'

The mentioned stepped forward. After a vague motion of a salute to Lisara, he spoke. 'After an Order raid on the building, a few men moved in and they seem to be looking for something.'

'Something?' she mumbled, now with an eyebrow raised as well.

'That's the issue.' Calem responded, 'We want to know what.'

'It could be the sword.' Nandla added, 'We have it on good authority that the Dragon has a sword he entices people with.'

'No one has seen the sword since the last time the Dragon was sighted... it would stand out.' Calem tapped the map again. 'The Order raided this place. I want to know why.'

'Well, you're not completely wrong...' Lisara mumbled, pulling in both men's attention.

'About?' they asked together.

She stood up straight, frowns and pouts gone. 'So where is this place and... where are we?'

*

He stood there. In the middle of the bedroom. He had not been in this room for quite some time, a thin layer of dust already settled on the furniture. But he didn't move.

The door was slightly ajar – escape would be easy should he want it, but he remained stoic, though it was quite to the contrary. His breathing had quickened, his eyes unfocused and still, his ears rang.

'Athrin.'

And then, silence. He suddenly found that he could breathe normally. His eyes scanned the room.

Everything in this room was perfect and neat. Not one thing out of place, and everything purposeful and tasteful. The bed and sheets were pulled neatly, the bedside tables packed with the essentials. A desk with a mirror and littered with neatly packed creams and cosmetics. In the corner stood a clotheshorse with a familiar navy blue jacket and a smaller purple one. In another corner was a chest of drawers adorned with picture frames and photos. None of them he could bear to focus on.

He realised now that he had been standing here motionless for quite some time. The feeling returned to his body and he remembered the box in his hand. Slowly, very slowly, he walked to the chest of drawers and then methodically and carefully he packed the photos away.

When only a single picture remained, he walked to the table and packed everything away, taking care not to break or damage anything.

He turned then to the closet and opened it. The familiar scent wafted back into the room. He needed to remain still for a time and collect his thoughts, then he removed every article of clothing that was not his and bagged them.

After some time, his task was done. Several bags and boxes sat in the corner ready to be taken away. Athrin sat on the corner of the bed and looked at the room, slowly taking it all in.

And then. It hit him. Utterly and completely.

He glared at the floor, angered by his own weakness. A few silent tears ran down his face. He felt ashamed. He felt weak. He felt helpless.

He felt alone.

Chapter VIII

Complacent Ire

A cry echoed through the hallway. A man ran from his aggressor, leaving his companions to their fate, but he tripped on his own feet and fell to the ground. And his attacker gained on him.

She stood over his body and with a quick flick of her sword she pierced his padded gear and ended the struggle. Lisara turned to the balcony and peered over the railing to the group down below. 'Any sign of the Dragon yet?'

Calem looked up to her after taking cover from the gunfire raining down from the floors above. 'Next floor!'

'Did you find something?' She leaned over the rail to get a better look.

'Next floor!' he cried again before joining his soldiers and returned fire.

With a solid 'harrumph', she pushed from the rail and strolled down the hallway towards the stairs. She wasn't sure what was going on here, a battle between Calem and his enemies, but whatever they were fighting over was unclear to her. What she did know was this should not have been her fight, and she was losing her patience.

On the floor above she found a few more soldiers and dispatched them quickly. One fell over the side when she threw her sword at him, with a quick flip of her wrist the sword came back to her and she was able to fell the other in the midst of the confusion. And then the gunfire came to an end.

Calem stormed up the stairs and approached her. She sat on the railing swaying her legs, and did not look at him as he came nearer. 'You took your time,' he said sternly.

Still, she did not look his way, instead gazing into the distance at something far away and probably more interesting for her at this moment.

'Your frivolous attitude is dismissible outside of combat but while we are fighting, I expect you to take it seriously.' He retained his stern tone, choosing to stand his ground and take this time to set her straight.

Now she looked at him. A quick turn fierce enough to knock over anyone not ready for it, she glared at him. 'I am not part of your little outfit, Calem.' Her hand found its way to the sword at her side. 'You would do well to remember that next time you lie to me.'

He did not falter. 'If you want our help, you're going to need to play ball.' Her grip tightening around the sword did not go unnoticed. 'Expecting something for nothing is foolish and selfish. You help us and we'll help you.'

She kicked from the railing and took a few steps away from him. With a quick flick, she whipped the sword through the air and rested it on her shoulder. 'Hurry up with your business so you can take me to the Dragon.'

*

The sun was setting. Athrin sat on the balcony rail and stared at the city. A cigarette in his mouth and a lot on his mind.

His journey to this point had been daunting, more so than he realised while walking the path, that realisation came during the respite. The time when he realised that he had not been living but was instead flailing wildly in a world that he did not agree with, but stayed because it was all he knew. But then she came. And at last, he had something to compare to the chaos, something better that was strikingly dissimilar and from then on it was all he ever wanted. And for a time, he had it. They had it, together.

And then it was over. Before it had a chance to truly begin. It was taken.

The burnt-out worm of ash fell from his mouth and tumbled on his leg as it slipped into the dark but he caught it in time, clenched it tightly in his hand. It burned his palm. The pain shot through his hand to his arm, if only for a moment. He didn't flinch. Instead, he stared at his clenched fist, almost curiously. Then he tossed the bud and ash into the ashtray and returned to staring at the city.

'Athrin,' a voice called.

Perhaps he was destined to be haunted, followed and called after for the rest of his days. But this was not the spectre, no, it took him a moment to recognise the voice. Lisara stood at the base of the wall around the premises looking up to him.

'I was not expecting you back so soon.' He noticed her demeanour was slightly lowered than normal; perhaps she was hoping to not return either.

'Whatever, Mr Righteous...' she snapped back but immediately withdrew herself, looking off to the side. 'Can I come up?'

He didn't mind. 'Sure.' He spun around ready to leap from the railing and get the door but instead she leapt to the railing and pulled herself up. He watched her struggle, reaching for a handhold. He offered his hand in one's stead. She took it and paused, looking up to him. There was no smirk on her face, no sign of a snide comment wrinkling her brow. It suited her better he thought, she was certainly beautiful.

'Do you mind...?' she began quietly, looking away from him. 'Help me up instead of starting at me.'

Quickly he hoisted her up and aided her climb over the railing where she brushed herself off and stood to face him.

'Thanks,' she said, quickly wiping her hand on his jacket. 'Ew.'

There it was. The missing snark. 'I will let you fall next time.'

'Preferable.' She peered at him through a leer and smiled. 'Looking down on everyone from your perch?'

Athrin rolled his eyes. He would not bother responding – whether she was deflecting or joking, he did not appreciate the sentiment. Instead, he left the balcony for the apartment. He was getting hungry.

She followed after a while, in silence. Perhaps she noticed his slight disdain.

'And so?' he began, rummaging through the freezer. 'What brings you back so soon?'

'Calem.' Her response started quietly, carefully. 'He can't find the Dragon.'

Nothing of note on ice, he turned to the pantry instead. 'He is the best to know where it might be.'

'It doesn't look like it.'

All he had left were some noodles; he hadn't been shopping in a while. He wasn't usually the one who did the shopping. 'It has only been a day.' He grabbed the noodles and flicked on the kettle. 'Give him some time.'

'I don't think time will help.'

The water boiled and steam started to rise out the plastic spout. 'Ask him about it. Perhaps you can help his search.'

'I did ask… he said some things. Asked me to help with things.'

The kettle shook and boiled and just as the light clicked off, Athrin lifted it and filled the noodle cup. 'Sounds like you are on top of it then.'

'Athrin!'

His hand paused. He looked up to see Lisara standing in the middle of the room with her hands in front of her. She appeared withdrawn and uncomfortable as if she was afraid of being in this room. He continued, filling the noodle cup then putting the kettle aside, then he circled the counter and stood in front of her. She watched him.

'Have you had something to eat?'

She looked from the cup of noodles in his hand to his eyes. 'No…'

He handed her one of the cups. 'Sit down. Eat.'

For a while, she still stood uncomfortably in the centre of the room. She watched Athrin take a seat and stir his noodles. She looked at the cup he gave her. She wasn't expecting him to facilitate her at all, let alone offer her food again.

'Lisara,' he called, bringing her back to attention. 'Please, relax. They are not that hot.'

She whipped to the couch opposite him and took a seat. Slowly, she mixed the noodles and tested the temperature. 'Thank you…'

'You are welcome,' Athrin replied. He watched her curiously; she still seemed uncomfortable and perhaps even nervous. He wondered what may have happened. This was unlike her. 'Something wrong with it?'

Lisara almost flinched, taking a moment to compose herself before she looked his way. 'No. It's fine.' She stirred the noodles and ate from the cup. 'Quite tasty.'

'Good,' he mumbled over a mouthful.

Silence loomed, the subtle sound of quiet slurping noodles and stirring. All the while, Lisara snuck a look at Athrin, watching him as if waiting for an opportune moment to interrupt him. But it never seemed to arise.

It was not guilt, nor was it a feeling of responsibility, but he was concerned for her to some extent. He sympathised with her. 'Where are you sleeping tonight?'

That question gave her pause, noodles dangling from her mouth. She slurped them up and smiled sheepishly. 'On this couch, I hoped…'

He shrugged. 'As long as you are quiet.' He dropped the fork into the empty cup and put it aside. 'And no, breakfast is not included.'

'Well, that's not fair.' She put her empty cup beside his. 'The sign outside said bed AND breakfast.'

'It lied.'

'How about a cup of coffee?'

'Only for paying customers.'

'I thought I was a VIP?' Lisara leaned a little forward, smiling as she twirled her hair around a finger.

'No, no.' He remained steadfast and stern. At times it was hard to tell when he was joking, but she could tell. 'Stowaway at best, invader at worst.'

'I thought we were a couple. Athrin, are you cheating on me?'

'So you stab all of your boyfriends?'

'Oh, this again! I made up for it with a kiss.' And she winked.

'It was the other way around, the stabbing made up for the kiss.'

She let out a fake gasp. 'How dare you, sir!' She threw an invisible stone at him. 'I'll have you know I am quite the catch. You should be grateful.'

'What was that for anyway?'

She looked away with a pout, perhaps even hiding something on her face. 'To get a read on you.' Then she looked at him again and smiled slyly. 'And to topple your defences.'

That was undeniable. Still strange, but she was quite strange. 'You could have just attacked me in my sleep.'

'I could have…' She considered it. 'But I also wanted to get a look at you, see what all the fuss was about.'

'Fuss?'

'Not overly impressed, to be honest.' She waved a hand at him. 'A lot of folks seem to harp on about you.'

That hurt a little. 'I would rather they did not.'

'Were you a big deal or something?'

He shook his head. 'Some people might say.' He shifted in his seat but remained neutral. 'But no, I did not do much.'

'Uh-huh.' She leaned forward and hoisted her legs to the couch. 'And that Calem wants to have your babies is just due to your handsome face?'

A sliver of a smile crossed his face for a moment as if he had thought of something, then it was gone. 'You think I am handsome, do you?'

'Pfffft.' She swayed backwards to cross her legs then leaned forward again. 'As if.'

'That would explain why you follow me around.'

'That's for the Dragon and you know it!'

'Are you blushing?'

A blade sang through the air. The edge of the sword stopped less than an inch from Athrin's neck. She held it fast and stared at him, appearing somewhat disgruntled. 'I might kill you in your sleep after all.'

'A little harsh…'

Athrin made to touch the blade, merely to shoo it from his neck. But just as his hand came near to the sharpened edge, she pulled it from him with an almost audible yelp. Both of them equally surprised by her reaction, she stared at him nervously and was again clearly uncomfortable. With a flick of her wrist, she tossed the blade aside and it disappeared. She then sat back down and huddled herself into a ball of silence.

This reaction was out of place. Assumptions could be made and he may even be correct, but he chose to ignore it. It was normal. When people found out who he was they were always cautious around him. Everyone. Except for one.

Athrin stood and took both cups to the bin. He rinsed and washed the forks.

'Athrin…' She stumbled over her words while she struggled to string her incoherent thoughts together. 'That wasn't what you think.'

'It is fine. Do not worry.'

Of course it was normal. Expected even. She was a Blade Bearer and he was a Blade Breaker, by merely touching the blade he would be able to tell its history and how it came to be, even its name, and her connection to it. And if he wanted, he could separate it from her very being and destroy it. He could destroy a piece of her soul. Of course it was normal.

'No… but…' She fell silent, burying her face behind her knees. It seemed she was unable to find a way to explain it. Perhaps she was even unsure herself.

Athrin circled around again and stood within her view. 'Shower is open, wear your own clothes this time. I will fetch a blanket for you.' After a few moments of not receiving a response, he left for the balcony.

He leaned against the railing, facing the apartment. With a tap to his palm, he separated a cigarette from the pack and put it to his mouth. A flick and a flash later smoke wafted around him. Inside he could spot Lisara. She was trying to see him through the glass and failing miserably at hiding it.

He smiled. He knew no one would see it.

This girl was a strange one, bobbing her head up and down and side to side, but he was hardly one to judge. Ever since she came tumbling into his life, the veil of monotony was disrupted. For a long time before all of this, he was something of a recluse, isolated and withdrawn. In fact, he could not remember a time before when he had spoken with someone at length like this. As adverse as he was to her and her mission, he knew somewhere in the back of his mind a little voice was telling him how good of a thing it was. In a way she had brought him back from the brink. Perhaps if it did not involve a gash across his chest and a teetering dance with death, it could be more fondly remembered. But it was not lost on him.

She leapt from the couch and tiptoed across the floor to the window, where she stood and peered through the glass, trying to spot him, though it seemed she could not. Her unkempt hair hung loosely around her in blonde streaks. She stood with her hands clasped behind her and leaned closer to the glass, her large, bright eyes darting in every direction.

He found himself staring at her. Admiring her tenacity and willpower, she had come all alone to this vast city, from possibly far away, all to hunt a mythical creature. And while her methods, or lack thereof, could be criticised, she seemed determined to see it through. Steadfast in who she was and what she needed to do. More than he could say of himself.

She had given up. Tiptoeing across the floor, she twirled at the corner and disappeared down the hallway. Hopefully his home would survive her.

*

Athrin tossed a blanket over her. Immediately, she wrapped it around herself and fell over the couch, squirming like a worm until she was comfortable.

'Well, goodnight.'

'Athrin! Tuck me in!'

He scoffed, taking the doorknob in his grasp and a moment to compose himself.

'Oooo, the forbidden door,' she muttered from across the room, her head poking up from the sheets. 'Not coming to bed yet, honey-bear?'

He remained at the door, his grip tightening. 'I am going to bed.' At last, he opened the door and stepped inside. 'Night.' Then closed himself in the darkened room.

It was dark and quiet. The faraway streetlamps and passing cars illuminated shapes and forms, enough for him to find his way. He pulled the sheets over himself and kept to the left side of the bed. His side. Then he emptied his mind as best he could and succumbed.

Chapter IX

Methodical Musings

The dense darkness enveloped him once again, uncomfortable and stifling. It was the same as before. The rumbling began again, drawing nearer and nearer to him and he could do nothing but wait for it. The massive form in the darkness peered at him once more but seemed more intrigued by him than before. It lingered for a longer time as if measuring his very being.

And then, it spoke. The voice seemed to come from every direction as if it was omnipresent, totally in control of this space.

'What do you seek?' The words were slow and enunciated with careful consideration; it felt as if every word commanded something of Athrin and demanded his complete attention.

But Athrin could not respond. The pressure around his formless self held him prisoner.

'Power?' The voice examined him. It did not need him to answer; it knew the answer. 'Knowledge?' It drew nearer to him, sensing something. 'Vengeance?'

This presence circled around Athrin, coiling around him like a massive serpent.

'I can give this to you.'

But Athrin denied this being a response, words or no, he denied it.

'Power to bend the will of those around you.' With the words came a vision, familiar faces and places, all of them warped and twisted, many of them dead. And at the head of this group, atop a metaphoric throne, was Athrin.

'Knowledge that would dwarf the greatest of libraries.' Another vision; this time it spanned thousands of years, sights and events he had only read about – many of them did not match what he had thought to know as history.

'Vengeance upon those who have wronged you.' This vision infected his mind, tore at his soul; it had struck true. It showed him what was, what could have been and what is. It sought to consume him, to overcome him. And it very nearly could have, but there was a light in this darkness. Perhaps it had been there this whole time, and he had only just noticed it.

Athrin wrenched himself from the beast's grasp. He would deny it still. He reached for the sliver of light, the one who was always there, the one who had shown him a better way.

*

His eyes snapped open. The nightmare was over. But what waited for him was arguably another.

Athrin lay on his side, facing the other side of the bed, which was occupied. Lisara stared at him. They were mere inches apart. She smiled at him with that mischievous grin. 'Finally awake, honey-bear?'

Athrin traced his hand, realising his fingers were touching the side of her face. Without the need for a gunshot, Athrin tore his arm away and shot from the sheets and bed in one movement. His back reached the wall. He could not retreat any further.

Lisara crept a little closer, lying over the bed, her legs swaying beneath the sheet. 'Aw, and we were just getting to the good part.'

'No,' he snapped, raising a hand as if he wanted to say more but retracted it when nothing came. He realised his attire, quickly grabbing a shirt and pulling it over his shoulders, then a pair of pants over his shorts. He turned away from her while he dressed. 'Why?'

'I got bored.' She rolled over to her back and reached out at the beams of light coming in from between the blinds. 'Also, the bed is so much more comfortable.'

The nightmare still clung to his mind; he could feel his nerves on end and his hands shaking, but he would need to hide this from her. Lest she strike him again. He was not sure what it meant; he needed time to think.

'You know you talk in your sleep?' she asked him, rolling her head to the side to glance his way and see the vague tinge of surprise on his face.

'I did not.'

'Very interesting mutterings,' she said with a precarious smile.

This was potentially bad; he needed an escape. 'Do not pry.' He left the room and made for the balcony, closing the sliding door behind him and took a deep breath.

Peace at last. He cast his gaze over the city. The dawn rose over the buildings. He lit a cigarette and leaned over the railing.

That nightmare replayed in his mind, over and over. It felt frighteningly real as if it was not merely a dream. Whatever it was or meant, one thing was clear; something was reaching out to him.

Behind him he could hear the door slide open and then closed, followed by the pitter-patter of bare feet. Lisara leaned over the railing beside him. 'Bad dream?'

'Something like that.'

'Seems like you have your own problems, besides tomorrow's spreadsheet.' She nudged his shoulder with hers.

He grumbled in response.

With a quick flick, she grabbed the cigarette from his mouth and pinched it between her lips, offering him but a wink in return.

Morning dew clung to the grass and a thin layer of frost melted and ran down the supports and railings. It was not overly chilly this morning. Athrin may have described it as 'fresh'. Lisara had once again pilfered clothes that were not hers – this time it was one of his shirts. Where she found the time to dig these out without him noticing was beyond him.

'So,' he began. 'What did I say?'

'Oh?!' That grin of hers returned as she tossed the remains of the cigarette to the ashtray. 'What do you think you said?'

Games, always the games. 'I asked because I do not know.'

'Guess.'

'Something along the lines of "stop stabbing the sofa and get a job"?'

'No, silly. Though, have *you* found a job yet?'

'Touché.'

'Come on, guess again. This is fun!'

'I would rather not play this game.' He pushed from the railing and made his way inside. 'I do not want to know anymore.'

She followed behind him. 'Kill-joy.'

*

'Calem.'

He ignored her.

'Calem.'

He guided his men through the plan, pointing here and there on the map sprawled out over the table.

'Calem.'

He drove a pin into a key point on the map, making sure they understood the precise position of it, and then traced the path with his finger for the umpteenth time.

'Calem.'

'What?!'

'I'm bored.'

'I don't care!' he snapped back, abandoning the map and his troops to stomp his way over to her. 'Go swing your sword at a light post or something.'

Lisara sat atop the ruined fountain, her sword on her lap and her knees raised high enough for her head to be perched on top of. The whole while, she did not look in his direction. 'Take me to this oracle you talked about.'

'Not now.'

'Now.'

'We have to make an appointment.' He threw his hands in the air, futilely displaying his frustrations. 'Besides, we may have a lead.'

She groaned audibly, loudly, even those on the upper floors peered over to be sure someone wasn't being tortured. 'This isn't another of those fake leads, is it?'

'No.'

'Because I've helped you plenty now.' Her head rolled to the other side. Perhaps her cheek was getting sore. 'Any more and you probably owe me dinner.'

'Someone spotted something unusual.'

'Dinner and a movie sounds pretty good actually. What's showing these days?'

'It was a thing with wings.'

Now he had her attention. Her head rolled over in his direction. 'Dragon-like wings?'

*

The phone rang.

Athrin tossed the washing into the basket and crossed the threshold. He stared at the ringing phone. It was not a number he recognised. Nevertheless, he lifted the receiver but said nothing.

'Is that Athrin?' a woman's voice called.

'Speaking.'

'It's Belle from…' she began, adding a lengthy acronym he did not care to remember. He said nothing in response, so she continued, 'I'm calling to offer you the job, are you still interested?'

Athrin stood in place. He felt nothing. Not relief, excitement, nor anxiety. Nothing. 'I am.'

'Excellent!' the voice exclaimed. 'When can you come in to finalise?'

'Whenever you need.'

'How's tomorrow?'

Civility. His quest. He needed to show it. 'Perfect.'

'Great stuff, Athrin. I'll see you tomorrow.'

'Thank you.'

The dull tone echoed through his ear. She had hung up already. Slowly, he cradled the receiver, but still remained in place.

Nothing.

He paced around the room. The washing was unfinished; he needed to hang it. The fridge was almost empty; he needed to restock it. Eventually, he found himself in the room, standing in front of the picture frame.

Civility. His quest. It was still important – that did not change. But everything else felt... hollow.

*

'I'll make you a deal, Calem,' she began, peering over his shoulder at the building in question.

'Oh boy. So excited.'

'You make an appointment with the Oracle' – half her sentence was accompanied by finger-quotes – 'and I'll go in there and kill whatever you want.'

Calem looked left and right, not spotting any suspicious onlookers. 'Tell you what; you kill it *first* and I'll get to it.'

'Nope.' She leaned against the streetlamp and folded her arms in protest.

They glared at each other. A contest for the ages. Calem would never admit defeat but he broke away first. 'Fine.' He turned to the side. 'Tilly.'

A woman appeared before him, emerging from the shadows, and stood at attention.

'Get in touch with our contact. Arrange a meet with the Oracle.' Just as Calem finished speaking, the woman nodded and vanished into the shadows. He turned to Lisara. 'There.'

With a smile denoting victory, she leapt from her reclined, yet defiant, position and stood ready. 'What am I looking for in there?'

'Not sure.' He joined her side. 'It has wings.'

'But it's not the Dragon?'

'Not sure,' he repeated, more clearly. 'The city is still intact, so that's doubtful.'

'Well, let's go.'

They crossed the street and approached the building. It was old and not quite decrepit but it would not pass many inspections; this end of town had many such places. They were the perfect places for people and other beings to take refuge.

'You seem to know what the Dragon can do. Did you cross paths with it before?' Lisara asked as they made their way further in.

Calem glanced over her head to check the streets again and ensure they weren't being watched. 'Once.' He opened a rusty gate and allowed her to walk before him. 'Few years ago.'

'And?'

'What do you mean "*and*"?' He hopped over a pile of trash on the path. 'It killed everyone. It splintered the Girdan to what we are now and caused the city to look to the Order in the panic. Letting them take control of the city.'

'I've been ignoring it for a while, but what's the deal with this "Order"? It's a stupid name.'

'Quite.' Calem stopped her with a hand. She glared at that hand and contemplated severing it from the arm. He peered around the corner, investigating the dark recesses. 'The Order is what they were referred to. Officially they are the Seceena City Military Force. And officially their goal is to prevent another uprising by the unmentionables of the city.'

'In other words: you.' She pushed past his arm and strolled through the courtyard, looking around for any signs of note.

'Us.' He hurried after her. 'Anyone with any connection to magical origins or something that is not seen as normal.' Once he was beside her, his eyes traced the apartments around them. It seemed quiet. 'Basically, witch hunters with guns and badges.'

'What does that make you?' She kneeled beside a stain on the ground. At first glance it could have been blood; not uncommon in these parts but still a clue.

'Peace keepers,' he said quickly, defensively, clearly a point of contention. 'We're here to deal with a problem threatening the people. The Order would rather burn this block to the ground.'

'Fire would be preferable...'

'Huh?'

'Don't move, Calem.' She stood quickly and moved closer to him. Her sword appeared in her hand. 'This place is a nest.'

*

Athrin paced the aisles, list in hand, and filled the basket one item at a time. There was no need to browse or compare; he knew what he was here for and it was always the same. The people around him investigated price tags, debated brands and saved a cent here and there, worthy to be sure, but he did not mind. He would always pass on the far side of others, squeeze past without them even knowing someone was there. This is how he dealt with people. He chose not to.

And finally, the last few items on the list, the exit in sight. The quicker the better. But then, 'Athrin?'

Out the corner of his eye he spotted the person. It was an unfortunate meeting. 'Rowley.'

The bearded Rowley stood with his own basket in hand, filled to the brim with soft drinks and junk-food. No judgement. 'Fancy seeing you here.'

Athrin dropped an item into his basket. Three items left, but they would have to go unticked today. 'Quite.'

Rowley raised his hands in defence. 'Come on, not my fault, man. Totally a coincidence.'

With a quick glance around the shop, Athrin came to the conclusion that this was not true. 'Right you are, Rowley. Goodbye.'

He stood in Athrin's path, blocking his exit. 'Don't be like that. Let's at least catch up.'

'I would rather we did not.'

'I would really rather we did.'

Athrin dropped the basket. The slam echoed through the store. The suddenly alert and wandering eyes of witnesses would buy him some time. 'I told you, Rowley, I am not working.'

'That's not what we've seen.' Rowley placed his basket on the ground, gently so as not to attract more attention. 'Saw you with a bearer. Broad daylight.'

Athrin swiped several items from the shelf beside him. The crash carried to the clerk who craned his neck to see what all the commotion was about. Several men in the store crossed their arms and wandered around, trying to remain inconspicuous.

'Giving directions.' He looked Rowley in the eye to make sure he understood. 'That business is done.'

'Why don't I believe you?'

'I do not care.'

'You should. It's a breach of your contract.'

With a quick shove, Athrin toppled a shelf. The tins and bags of produce scattered across the floor. The clerk left his station and moved to investigate.

'This does nothing for you, man. Buys some time at best.' Rowley raised his hand in the air. Several people in the store immediately made for the exit. 'We'll be in touch.'

'Get out of my store!' the clerk yelled, shooing both Athrin and Rowley with his hands. 'Look what you've done! I'll call the police!' He shooed some more. 'Get out!'

*

Calem crouched behind an old couch, just in time, as a sword flew through the air and embedded into the wall near him. Lisara sped past, grabbing the blade and running off towards the howling and shouting. She seemed to be enjoying herself, twirling and leaping with every attack and swipe of her blade. The twisted and deformed creatures did not stand for long.

He could hear her laughing in the distance. 'That girl is crazy.' He shot up from cover and gave chase, kicking a surviving beast as he hurried down the hall after her.

The beast roared loudly as Lisara approached. Backed into a corner, it seemed to be out of places to hide from her. Some would debate on who was the monster here. Its form was humanoid, fangs where teeth would be and razor-sharp claws for fingers, long brown hair the only remaining piece of the masquerade.

Calem caught up to her, slightly out of breath. 'Is that it?'

'The matriarch?' Lisara did not take her eyes off her prey. 'No, smaller one. No sign of the mother.'

'Okay, well…' Calem stepped forward and addressed the creature. 'Vampiric denizen, you have violated the parley and we are here to put you down.'

The creature's panic regressed while it listened to Calem's words.

'I was not expecting… this…' He motioned to the grizzly surroundings of blood and bone. 'Evidence of the poor job we've been doing.'

'Can I kill it?' Lisara interrupted, her fingers tingling with impatience.

In that moment the creature leapt at them in a final bid for victory, only to be cut down by Lisara's sword in one quick and clean motion. Blood sputtered from its mouth as it seemed to be cackling at them. The cold dead eyes locked on Lisara.

'Disgusting.'

It spat before falling silent.

With a quick whip, Lisara cleaned the blood from her sword and stepped closer to the carcass. 'I think I'll take that dinner after all.' She looked at Calem, a streak of blood on her cheek, and smiled. 'Movie, optional.'

His hands flailed wildly as he sought words he could not find. All he could utter was: 'You… are crazy.'

She raised her head with pride. 'Like a fox.'

'Catherine?!' a quiet voice came from the debris. Immediately, Lisara poised herself to strike but Calem stopped her. A man frantically crawled his way to the corpse of the creature. He was covered in filth and his clothes tattered. Clearly, his mind was lost. He cupped the beast's face in his hands and stared at it. 'What's happened…' he stammered. 'Speak to me…'

Calem fought with Lisara as she tried to inch her way to the man at sword-point. He won the squabble and she retreated a few steps with a pout.

'Sir…?' he called gently to the man as he approached him.

But the man did not respond.

'The vampire's cattle. There may be more here somewhere.' He turned away from the man and to Lisara. 'Hang around till the reinforcements get here, then you can go… wherever it is you go.'

'Fine.' She tossed her blade into the air. It disappeared before reaching Calem's head, then she wandered around, examining the grizzly scenery. 'Maybe a buffet.'

*

Before long, the rundown building was busy with Calem's people. They searched each room, each dark corner, for any surviving creatures or people, but it seemed there was only the one survivor.

Calem approached Lisara after finding her sitting in the middle of a courtyard on what was left of a bench, surprised that she hadn't slipped away already. 'I thought you'd take the opportunity to skedaddle.'

She turned to him as he approached, brushing stray hair behind her ear, and watched him closely until he came to a standstill a few feet from her. 'I want a time and place before any skedaddling happens.'

'Look, Lisara, no buffet…'

'The Oracle, dumbass.'

'I'll let you know as soon as I hear back from them, I'll keep my word. After what you did here today, I have to.' He smiled, anticipating her next comment. 'No. No buffet.'

She pouted loudly, leering at him with such intensity she hoped he would catch on fire. 'I hate you.'

'Fair enough.' He leaned against the bench, and a little closer to her. 'Thanks for today.'

She nodded, turning away from him and looking off into the distance, as if someone far away had suddenly called her name.

Still, Calem kept his focus on her, something building within his eyes. 'Say, Lisara…' He stared at her, considered, and planned. 'Would you…'

'Athrin used to do stuff like this for you?' She didn't look his way. 'Back when you were besties?'

'I don't really want to talk about him behind his back.'

'I'll shut up about the buffet?'

Calem thought in silence for a moment. Abandoning something when he weighed the consequences, and ultimately decided it wouldn't hurt for her to know. It may even help his own goal. 'He was not really ever with us.' He let out a long sigh. 'He left the Order under conditions; namely, that he would remain neutral and not get involved with their or our business. Both sides agreed.'

'Well, that's not very interesting.'

'What do you want to hear then?'

'I want…' She thought, structuring her request. She knew this chance would not come again, and she felt she needed to know. For herself, not for any mission or objective – even after all this time she had been with Athrin, she knew nothing about him. 'I want to know why so many people are fighting over him.'

Chapter 8

The Last Drop

Silence loomed. Even the dripping tap was drowned out in the vacuum.

'Can I—'

'Quiet!' she yelled.

Lisara stood over Athrin, their eyes maybe an inch apart, a very visible furl on her brow.

It had been several minutes already. Several more passed. Awkwardly.

'Just do not—'

'I don't see it,' she cried, pushing him back to the couch and letting go of his collar. She paced around the room angrily. 'Lies, must be lies.'

He did not care, mostly, but today's events brought a lot into question. 'Looking for something?'

'Well… the Dragon.'

That did not bode well.

'But right now, I'm fact-checking.'

A little better.

She swung to look at him again, an accusatory finger aimed in his direction. 'You're a meek puppy dog, that's all.'

'That might hurt…'

'But if you're not a docile little cub, then you are actually capable.'

'Thanks?'

'Damn it, Athrin!'

He raised his hands in surrender and looked around the room. Perhaps some sort of salvation was in sight, hidden until now. It was not. 'Do you want to start from the beginning?'

'Whatever!' She sat opposite him, crossing her legs and folding her arms in tight frustration. 'Doesn't matter, going to see that Oracle person soon.'

'You have not been already?'

'No!' she exclaimed suddenly, and he immediately regretted asking as she continued. 'I've been running around and working my taut little behind off for Calem and his clubhouse.'

'Doing what?'

Another question he regretted. 'Stuff!' She threw her hands up, now more annoyed as she summarised the past week. 'He yells and points a lot. And then lies a lot, like how he won't treat me to the dinner he promised!'

'Wow. Douchebag.'

'Right?!' She collapsed into the couch, seemingly having spent all of her energy. 'Anyway…' she grumbled, looking in his general direction. 'How was your day, honey-bear?'

He decided to humour her. 'Got the job. Starting tomorrow.' He would leave out some details though.

'Oh, that's good.' The enthusiasm spilled over. 'You won't be a deadweight anymore.'

Something of a chuckle escaped him. 'I suppose not.'

'Look at us.' Lisara wrenched from her reclined position with some difficulty. 'You, back to your fruitless meandering. Me, about to see some or other psychic to tell me where a deadly creature is hiding.'

Obviously, she seemed frustrated, and maybe even a little angry. Athrin sympathised. 'I am sorry, Lisara.'

Her neck craned towards him; at last something interesting was happening.

'I would help if I could.' And he meant it. He had come to understand, and even relate to, what she was going through. Had he the ability, the freedom, he might have helped her, because it was a noble cause and it was the right thing to do. He had been taught to see this.

'I get it, Athrin.' She rolled over to her side, staring at nothing. 'The Order would send the hounds if they saw you running around on this side of the fence.'

So she knew. But she still misunderstood and for some reason, it was important to him that she know the reason. He wasn't sure why.

'I am not afraid of that.' He paused, gathering his thoughts and stringing together a way to explain it. 'I cannot because I made a promise.' Another pause, this time for a different reason. 'I promised to be done with that life.'

Silence for a time. The ambience of the city outside took over the room, far off cars sped by, quiet chatter of the neighbours preparing for bed and somewhere a siren or two.

'Was it Amber?'

A chill ran through his entire body. Athrin could feel his heart quicken and his breath become heavier. He looked at her, startled that she knew that name.

Lisara watched him from where she lay. 'You mumble in your sleep.'

He turned away, trying fiercely to calm the throbbing in his chest.

'Is she the girl in the photo?'

Though he did not respond, Lisara could clearly see the effect it had on him. And through caution or curiosity, she would not relent.

She sat up and watched him closely. 'Was she the one that turned you away from your life?'

'Don't.'

'Did she put all these things in your head? Tell you to stop using your talent?'

'Stop it.'

Lisara leaned closer. She would keep going; she could see something struggling to rise to the surface. 'You're clearly unhappy here, Athrin. I can't see how you'd choose this.'

'I didn't...'

'Then why?' She could not see his face. 'Why give up on everything?'

'She *was* everything!' He stood suddenly, knocking the table with his leg. A mug fell over and rolled to the floor. 'None of that bullshit out there mattered – I gave it up so we could have a future.' He clenched his fists tightly at his side, his knuckles turning white, lost in rage. 'She didn't make me do it. She wanted me to help people but I wanted to be there for her. All I wanted...' He paused. Stopped completely. He realised for the first time that he had been yelling, that he had snapped. He retreated a foot.

Lisara was taken quite aback. She had never seen such a reaction from him; it was the most he had ever told her about what went on in his head. As shocked as she was, she was perhaps more intrigued by it.

'I... I'm...' His feet hit the couch. He could not retreat further this way. 'I am sorry... I...'

She watched him intently, fascinated by what she was seeing in him as he hurried to fix the walls and plug the cracks. She had perhaps not given him enough credit. He may have been interesting after all.

Quickly, he left, throwing the balcony door open and closed again behind him, then vanished into the darkness.

Lisara's eyes followed him into the dark. She watched as he lit a cigarette and slid to the floor in a corner of the balcony. She could not hold back the sliver of a smile.

*

A cloud of smoke floated around him. He scrunched another cigarette into the floor, adding to several other crumpled stubs around him. Athrin had been here for quite some time; he was unsure for how long exactly. He had stopped paying attention to it.

With a glance inside, he could see Lisara was still asleep. Every now and again she would toss or turn, but remained still otherwise. She had brought something out of him, something he thought had been dealt with but clearly, it was still there. With enough prodding. He was not angry with her; she had done nothing wrong. His outburst was due to his own weakness. A weakness, that's what it had to be.

Hoisting himself up by the railing, he stood and quietly entered the apartment. He made for the bedroom and was sure to lock the door behind him. He was not in the mood for any more surprises.

*

'Good to see you, Athrin.' The woman shook his hand just as he passed the threshold. 'Glad you came early. We have a lot to do.'

Good news, he thought. The busier the better. 'Thank you for having me, Belle.' He straightened the strap of the bag on his shoulder and took a look around the office. 'I am eager to get started.'

'Great attitude!' she exclaimed. 'This way, we'll start with your desk.'

They walked through the offices, many people quietly going on about their own business, a few huddled together discussing or chatting. Seemed like a nice place, he thought.

'And here we are.' She turned to him and presented an empty spot. It was at the back and away from the others, a perfect spot for him. 'Get comfortable, I'll be back soon and we'll get the rest of your paperwork ticked off.' She smiled at him before hurrying off in another direction.

Athrin took a look around; it was quiet back here. He swung his bag off his shoulder and placed it neatly on the table. Then he took a seat in the comfortable-looking chair, which it was, and rolled to the table. Taking a moment to soak it all in. This could work.

*

'Lisara,' Calem called, searching high and low through his headquarters. He checked all the usual hiding places and spots where she would normally be, but there was no sign of her.

'Lisara!' he called a little louder now and walked towards the kitchen, the last place he hadn't checked. Sure enough, he found her here, arm-deep in the cookie jar. 'Would it kill you to answer me?'

She looked at him, arm still in the jar and a round biscuit in her mouth. 'Huh?' she mumbled.

'I've been looking for you.'

She snatched a handful and put the jar back into the hiding place she had discovered it in. 'I've been here all morning. Someone hid the cookies again.'

'Yeah, from you.' He snatched one from her hand and stuffed the whole thing into his mouth. 'We have an appointment with the Oracle today. We should leave soon.'

'Oh.' She circled around him and sat at the table, relaxing against the chair. 'Don't worry about it.'

Perhaps she misheard him, he thought. 'The Oracle will see us. Don't you want to ask about the Dragon?'

'Meh, not too fussed.'

Maybe this was some kind of game again. He sat opposite her and tried to catch her eye, and her focus. 'I thought you were eager to see the Oracle?'

'Who?'

'The Oracle.'

'Of what?'

'Of... stuff... I don't know!' He threw his arms in the air. 'What's happening?! Don't you want to go?!'

'Nah, not particularly.' She munched on another cookie.

He was tempted to pull some hair out. 'Too bad!' He stood quickly and slammed the table. 'I've made an appointment and we're going.'

'Hang on...' She finished off a cookie and stood calmly, dusting her hands over the table. 'I want another cookie.'

Quickly, Calem rushed past her and grabbed the jar from the hiding place. He held it tightly and glared at her. 'If you want these, you have to come with me.'

'Calem… you don't want to do this.'

'Oh, I do.' He pulled one out from the jar and tossed it at her. She caught it and immediately started chewing on the corner. 'You can have another at the car.'

'Fine,' she mumbled over the crumbs. 'Chocolate!'

*

Several hours had passed. For Athrin they were mostly uneventful; he filled in some of his paperwork and got himself accustomed to his new space. The pitter-patter and clicking of keyboards was a quiet ambience on the floor. Everyone seemed rather quiet. He appreciated this.

Suddenly, he could hear footsteps, different from the norm, hurried and urgent. Belle appeared from around a corner. She looked at Athrin with an expression matching her stride. 'Athrin…' she began nervously and in a hushed tone. 'There are some men here to see you.'

'A meeting already?' he asked with a forged smile. He knew it and the question was pointless.

She leaned a little closer. 'It's the police.'

Civility.

Athrin would play the part. He followed Belle to the front and met with the policemen, two men, dressed smartly in their navy blue uniforms, their badges and weapons displayed clearly.

There were no words for this, as he had nothing to offer. He would conform, for he had no reason not to. He followed the men outside and to the car waiting for him. Without hesitance, he entered and let them drive him away. He knew why this was happening. He knew where he was going and who would be there. None of these things mattered to him now. He thought that perhaps it would have had a more profound effect on him – this potentially ruined his new job – but he surprised himself. He felt nothing. He gazed out the window at the city as it passed him by, the zombies wandering the streets and the buildings seemed so at peace.

His mind was afire with questions, not to his circumstance but to his reasons. He wondered on the chain of events that led him to this point, the string of fate that he ran along helplessly. As with everything in his life, he felt only as if he was along for the ride.

Not long after departing, the car came to a stop at the foot of a building, the police precinct. He followed the officers inside and to a small room where they sat him down. They did not restrain him, there was no need, he offered no resistance.

This room was small, a table in the centre and a chair on either side. He sat facing the mirror which he knew was one-way. He could only guess as to who would be on the other side and he may have even been right. There was a camera in one corner. The absence of a blinking light led him to believe it was switched off, and that much would make sense; no one would want this to be known.

'Athrin.' The door opened and a woman entered, taking her time to close the door and turn to him slowly, a self-assured smile stretched across her face. 'You're a hard man to find.'

He did not recognise her but her uniform undoubtedly identified her as someone from the Order, a high-ranking member.

Slowly she strolled around the room, ending her pace at the chair opposite Athrin, but she did not take a seat. 'Luckily for us you decided to take a job. Right under our noses.'

Her badge betrayed her as a sergeant, with the name 'Hanson' embroidered on the shirt just above the clip. He noticed the empty holster at her side. No doubt the good graces of the police only extended so far.

'I'm sure you can figure out why you're here,' she said, still with a smile from ear to ear. Now she took a seat and crossed her arms over the table. 'Rowley sends his greetings.'

'Okay,' Athrin responded simply. He did not see the need to engage her any more than he had to; this manner of interrogation was nothing new to him.

She took a moment, waiting for him to say something more, but he did not. 'To be frank, I am not that impressed. I've heard stories about the infamous Equaliser Athrin, but now that I got to see you...' She ended the sentence with a condescending shrug.

She sought to rattle him. He leaned forward slightly. 'Would you like an autograph?'

'Cute.' She sneered at him and the smile steadily began to decline. 'So, after breaching your contract, that's your attitude?'

'Sorry, should I leave?'

She slammed the table. Athrin did not flinch.

'I don't think you appreciate the gravity of your situation, Athrin.' She stood and wandered over to the mirror, all the while watching him in the reflection. 'You're in a lot of trouble.'

'I do not think so.'

'No one cares what you think.' She spun around to him. 'You went against the arrangement, and you picked poorly.'

'Grievances?'

She slammed the table again, louder this time, but still could not generate a reaction from Athrin. 'I don't think you understand.'

'No, ma'am, it is you who does not understand.'

She made to speak again, to interject and correct him, but he spoke over her, without the need to speak louder. The severity was clear in his tone and his words.

'Your detail has made a mistake. I have not broken my arrangement, you have. I do not know why you decided to execute this order without your superior knowing about it, but that was a mistake.' He motioned towards the door. 'Someone is on their way here, of higher rank than you, and they will most likely relieve you of duty.'

She seemed surprised, sprinkled with anger. 'How dare you. How can you possibly—'

He interrupted again, knowing already what she would say. 'Because your Commander would never have allowed this. It goes higher than you.' Athrin's demeanour softened; the mood in the room returned to what it was. 'No offense.'

After a moment of uncomfortable silence, she straightened herself and made to resume her interrogation, but something else stopped her again, this time it was knock on the door.

First, she turned to look at him, surprise turned to shock, the anxiousness and doubt clearly taking hold. Then she stood slowly and answered the door.

A man stood in the doorway. His mighty frame filled it from side to side and top to bottom. He glared down at her. His face was cold and hard, a scar across a cheek, short grey hair spiked the top of his head and stubble lined the collar of his coat.

'Commander Artos…' She stammered while the realisation set in, Athrin's words came to fruition. 'I…'

'Hanson.' He growled. 'Get out of here – wait outside.'

Without any response, she left quickly and closed the door behind her, leaving Athrin and this man alone.

He turned to Athrin then walked closer to the table.

Athrin stood, and out of a remembered respect, he saluted the man. 'Commander,' he greeted.

'As you were, Athrin,' he mumbled. 'Always the disciplined and proper. I miss that.' He then turned to the mirror and tapped twice on the glass. Athrin knew if anyone was still on the other side, that signal was their last warning to vacate. 'Good to see you again.'

Athrin stood normally, his arms crossed behind his back. 'And you, sir.'

'I heard about what happened.' He turned to Athrin and approached a few steps. 'Know that you have my condolences,' he said and stretched out his hand.

'Thank you.' Athrin shook his hand, Artos' powerful grip always enough to give him pause.

'Now, this whole affair.' Artos shoved the chair under the table, visibly a little angrier now. 'My apologies for Hanson's actions. She and her entire unit will be reprimanded.'

Athrin shook his head. 'Not necessary, sir. I am to blame as well.'

'Honest, honourable.' Artos shot Athrin a look capable of passing right through him. 'They don't make them like you anymore.' He threw his arm out to the side towards the door. 'Regardless, I will not tolerate insubordination.'

Athrin knew as much.

'And?' He focused on Athrin again. 'Your business with that Blade Bearer?' His gaze was cold and calculating, as if watching Athrin's every movement.

'It has nothing to do with the Girdan,' Athrin said simply. He would need to choose his words carefully.

'This person's affiliation?'

'I did not inquire.'

'Motive?'

'I could not pretend to know.'

'Is Calem still the head of those riffraff?'

'I cannot say.'

'Why not?'

'I prefer to remain neutral. Sir.'

'Good answer.' Artos may have smiled, too small a detail to be sure. He turned away from Athrin and checked his watch. 'As I thought, there was no need for this.' He paced around the room, his hands behind his back, his posture – perfect. 'I will do what I can to make this disappear with the authorities. My hope is that it will not affect you.'

'Thank you, sir.'

'Then we can put this behind us.' He moved to the door. He had decided the conversation was coming to a close. 'Good to see you again, Athrin. Do not worry. We will deal with this Blade Bearer.'

That last comment gave Athrin pause, which was noticed. He ignored the gesture to exit the room. 'Deal with?'

'Indeed.'

'Why?'

Artos' brow furled into a prominent frown. 'We cannot have a rogue Blade Bearer running around the city, Athrin, especially not at this time.' He directed his narrowed scowl towards Athrin. 'I'm sure you know this.'

'She is not a threat to the Order. There should be no need.'

'Athrin.' Artos clasped the doorknob tightly in his hand; the door's hinges may have even creaked. 'If I didn't know any better, I'd think you're trying to get involved.'

Now Athrin matched his glare, his mask of a bygone professionalism cast aside. 'You should leave her alone, Commander.'

Artos noticed this change, could see it in Athrin's eyes, something that was never there before. He opened the door and gave Athrin a final sneer before leaving. 'I will do whatever I damn well please. This is my city.'

*

The room was large and well lit. From the outside, one would expect something more run-down and decrepit but perhaps that was the intention. The tapestries were ornate and impeccable, royal red colours complemented with gold linings. To one side of the room was a bar and kitchen, out of the way and neatly kept. On the other side was what appeared to be a formal meeting room with large comfortable couches and at the head of these stood a single chair, raised a foot above the others atop a podium. No one else was here yet.

'Tacky,' Lisara muttered. Almost immediately, Calem shushed her lest anyone overhear. She wandered around and inspected the room some more.

'Calem.'

He turned to the speaker and shook his hand. The man was about the same height and build as he, and he knew him well enough. 'Zieg,' he greeted politely. 'How are you?'

Zieg nodded simply. 'Have a seat. She is on her way.'

'Oh no, no.' Calem reached out for Lisara, trying to lasso her closer through sheer will. 'We won't be long. I wouldn't want to intrude any further.' Lisara did not answer his calls. 'Lisara!' he whispered fiercely, and only then did she trot closer.

'Who's this?' she asked while giving Zieg a curious look-over.

'Zieg is one of the Oracle's guards.' Calem leaned closer to her and whispered in her ear, 'He's a Blade Bearer too.'

Lisara raised an eyebrow as she examined Zieg's person. 'No, he's not.'

'This way.' Zieg guided them closer to the one side of the room and as soon as they approached, a door behind the chairs opened up as two more people entered the room. One was dressed similarly to Zieg, also a guard; the other was striking to behold. It was a woman with long blonde, almost silver, hair that flowed around her like a silk veil as she walked. Her lengthy gown followed her as she seemed to float through the air with every step; her presence alone seemed to lighten the room and put those present at ease. Save for one.

'I forgot my sunglasses…' Lisara mumbled.

Calem nudged her to be quiet and bowed in this woman's presence. 'Lady Alari, it is an honour to be in your presence again.'

The woman looked over to him and smiled warmly, shooing the guards around her if they got too close. Apparently, she did appreciate the pomp and circumstance. When she spoke, her words were as ethereal as she, her tone gentle and soothing. 'Calem.' She did not sit, but stood as they did. 'It is good to see you again. The winds have been favourable to guide you here once more.'

'At your mercy, milady.' Calem lowered his head further. 'You led us through a crisis.'

'As a storm that passed through the city, leaving no home untouched, no street clear.' She looked around the room before resting her eyes on him again. 'The wounds still sting, for some more than others.'

'It is as you say, milady.' Calem raised his head slightly, 'I shall not keep you long. I have come today on behalf of another, seeking your guidance.'

'I shall do all I can, Calem. It is the shepherd's role to guide, not to lead astray.'

'Um, duh.'

Alari looked at Lisara now, as if only noticing her for the first time. From then, her gaze did not leave her.

Calem nudged Lisara again. 'This is she, milady, one that seeks your council.'

Alari said nothing, watching Lisara with a neutral expression.

'Not really, I guess...' Lisara fiddled with the hem of her top, looking around the room.

The uncomfortable air in the room did not go unnoticed. Calem anxiously stepped forward, 'She's a Blade Bearer from... somewhere... and has come to this city, hunting the Dragon.'

There was a noticeable shift in the room, the guards visibly different and increasingly wary.

'She believes it is in the city, and I thought you may be able to help her find it.'

'To what end?' one of the guards asked.

'Well...'

'Only the sorceress can harm it,' another said.

Calem looked at Lisara, waiting for some reaction, but she returned nothing besides complete disinterest. 'Lisara...' he whispered. 'Show them you're a bearer.'

She rolled her eyes and with a sigh, the sword appeared in her hand. She rested the tip on the floor and leaned on the pommel.

Calem made to speak again but Alari spoke over him, her tone more serious than anyone in the room had ever heard. 'Why have you come here?'

Lisara shrugged. 'I was promised cookies.'

The room was silent until Calem nudged her again. 'What are you talking about?! Aren't you after the Dragon?!' He looked at Alari desperately. 'She's after the Dragon!'

Alari's attention had still not left Lisara, caution and disdain clear in her eyes. 'The Dragon walks with her.'

CHAPTER XI

WHEN THE RAIN COMES

The door closed behind him, leaving him in the embrace of a darkened room. Slowly his eyes adjusted to the dark and shapes emerged from the shadows. Athrin stood at the threshold and looked around the room. His home. His refuge.

He walked slowly across the room, running his fingers along the familiar objects and surfaces, picturing their past, picturing the one who came before. His eyes came to a stop at the door to the bedroom. And there he stood for a time. A long time.

'What's on your mind?' a voice asked him. Her voice. She had returned to haunt him. To antagonise him. To comfort him.

Athrin did not turn to face her; she wasn't real. He did not respond. There was no one there, but he stood in place and waited.

The dark recess of the apartment hummed with sounds of memories, laughter, heartache and adoration. 'You didn't let go.' She moved around the room, instantly from the kitchen, preparing a meal, to the couch, passing the time, and everywhere in between. Her days portrayed.

He opened the door to the bedroom and entered carefully. He followed one foot after the other until he found himself in front of the photo. The image barely visible in the dark.

She may have been standing behind him. An inch away, her hand clutching the back of his shirt, her head lowered. 'It makes me sad to see you this way.'

He had heard those words once. The circumstances much different to this but the dull pain in his chest the same. He did not like it.

'You can't go on like this,' she may have said. In his mind's eye he could still picture her around the room, rummaging through the closet for something to wear, fiddling with her makeup, lying beneath the sheets fast asleep.

But he remained.

A quiet sobbing came from a corner of the room. Chatter surrounded him, memories long forgotten trailed into his mind. One chaining to another in a sequence he could not stop. All he could do was close his eyes and wait. And hope for it to pass.

Maybe she laughed. Rare in the last few months. 'Why won't you let go?'

'How can I?'

There was a sudden shriek; it turned his stomach. 'Athrin!'

He felt a weight collapse onto him from every direction. Suffocating him. It was suddenly cold. Still, he did not move. One thought led to another, swirling inwards and outwards, one with no end. With each spiral the memories became distorted, twisted and corrupted. Indistinguishable from his nightmares.

'Athrin.' The voice was quiet again. Almost a whisper, barely emerging from the rattling in his mind, but he could hear it. He could never deny her call.

His hand crept to his head and he grabbed a handful of hair, his teeth clenched. His mind was on fire. So many voices, so many memories, so much he wished to forget. 'I can't...' he muttered broken words. 'I can't do this without you.' He let out a long, slow breath he didn't know he had kept held.

And then, he saw her. He could picture her, more real than any of the silhouettes before. She was standing in front of him, her hand on the side of his face, and in that instant the pressure lifted. His mind purged and clear, he could feel the warmth return to his body and he could breathe again. She smiled at him. 'You can.'

'I can't.' He fell to his knees. She followed him. 'I've tried.' His breath quickened and he fought to correct it. 'I made a mess of it. All of it.'

'You did.' She smiled, may have even chuckled.

'See?'

'I see you clinging to something broken.' She spoke gently, cupping his head in both of her hands, and brought his eyes up to meet hers. 'I see you struggling to piece it together.'

'I'm trying to.'

'Don't.'

He watched her; she seemed so real, even the way she smiled when he didn't understand something that seemed so simple.

'Even if you piece it together, it will never be the same.' She raised his head slightly, bringing them closer together. 'Make something else.'

'Amber.' He moved his hand, inching nearer to her. 'I am so scared of losing you.'

'Athrin...' She tilted her head to the side, her smile and expression filled with everything she felt for him, then a tear ran down her face. 'You already did.'

*

It was there, in the dark recesses. It watched, and it waited. Time was of no consequence. Time was abundant. All it needed to do was wait, only to wait until the last speck fades. Until it bleeds out. Then it steps forth, reveals just enough of itself that the prospect may appear inviting. Until then, it will wait.

*

With plastic bag in hand, Athrin left the store. He had finally checked the items off of the list and could stock the fridge.

He stopped as he came to a red light and joined the few people here already patiently waiting to cross the street. He did not look at any of them; he was not in the mood for any conversation today. It had been three days since he lost his new job.

'*Complications.*' That's what he was told. Though he was expecting it, after being dragged away by the police, falsely or otherwise, it was still an unwelcome predicament.

He checked the light. Still red.

Standing here with nothing to do, it dawned on him that he had spent these past few nights alone. He looked left, then right, lest he summon the inconvenience. Still, Lisara was oddly absent. Perhaps she had made progress on her Dragon hunt. Maybe, just maybe, he had seen the last of her.

Somehow, he didn't fancy that thought.

Prompted by a click and musical tone, Athrin joined the herd and they crossed the street, and so he continued home, all the while now thinking of that girl who had once stabbed him.

As he turned the corner, he prepared himself, expecting to see her in the usual spot at the stairs, only there was no one here. Strangely relieving.

With a twist, a kick and a slide, he had entered his home, de-shoed his feet and stocked the fridge. A sigh helped him relax and mould himself to the couch. He took a moment to look around and listen. Silence. Just what he needed.

But there was a nagging feeling in the back of his mind. The empty space on the couch opposite him, with the neatly folded blanket, taunted him. He tried to ignore it. A battle he was losing. He thought back to his meeting with Artos and considered again the gravity of his words.

Athrin wondered what had become of Lisara. The ill intentions of Artos alone was enough to worry but he could not help but feel something else was amiss. He had this feeling for a while already; it was something he had not been able to shake. It wouldn't hurt to go for a walk, he thought.

*

The city was bustling with excitement. Posters, banners, decorations, all preparing for a special visitor to the city. Athrin gave the area a wide berth. There were too many people around there for his liking. He remembered hearing of this visitor before – the President was coming to the city. He recalled the map in Calem's abode. More than that, he ignored it.

His slow stroll brought him to the corner of Birch Street. While he had no intention of going into the quarters of Calem and his associates, he knew it would not take long for someone to emerge and check on him. And he was correct.

A man emerged from the alleyway and approached Athrin immediately. 'Master Athrin,' he greeted.

It made Athrin wince. He disliked the titles. 'Just Athrin, please.'

'Of course, sir.' He bowed his head. 'We were not expecting you. What brings you here?'

'A query. You do not have to answer.' With a glance left and right, Athrin checked the surroundings for onlookers. 'Has the Blade Bearer been through here lately?'

'She has, yes.'

That bode well.

'But a few days ago, Calem ordered for all teams to be on the lookout for her.'

That less so.

'Calem is out at the moment, with a team combing the city. I'm not sure what happened.'

Probably bad.

'Master Athrin?'

Another wince. 'Let Calem know I stopped by.'

'Oh, that's okay, Master Athrin. I have already sent word of your presence, as I was ordered.'

Definitely bad.

'I apologise if this has caused you any inconvenience.'

'No.' Athrin waved a hand and began to walk off. 'You do what you need to.'

'Where can Calem find you, Master Athrin?'

'I will find him.'

*

This spot in the city was a quiet, secluded area. Something of a park, with a single bench near the only tree and a small shop at the back which appeared to have gone out of business.

It was the near-centre of the city and the perfect place if one needed to begin a search. And it was where he began. Athrin stood in the middle of the open area. He swept his gaze upon the familiar sights and wondered if he would spot someone he recognised. But he was alone. He found himself staring at the tree. It was an old tree, probably older and taller than any of the buildings around it, and its significance was not lost on him.

Just like he had been taught, he placed his hand on the trunk of the tree and focused. His senses began to heighten and grow. This place aided in the process and he began to see the signs invisible to most people who did not have the sense, and even then not all had the ability. It took a few moments for his senses to adjust and begin his search, reaching out as far as he could.

And there it was. A ripple. It was incredibly subtle; he would never have noticed it had he not spent enough time with her. But he was sure. His hand left the tree – he had a destination now. Before that, however, he had a guest.

A woman stood not far from him. She was neatly dressed and presented herself confidently. Her long, dark brown hair was tied loosely in a ponytail behind her head. She watched him cautiously.

He recognised her, although he had last seen her years ago, yet by her reaction it seemed she did not recognise him.

'Not a lot of people come here,' she said simply while moving slowly and carefully to subtly block the way out.

He would have to choose his words carefully as this woman's presence was troublesome at this moment. 'I was hoping to see an old friend.' He chose poorly.

Her emerald-green eyes locked onto him, a bad sign, but she smiled and began to slowly walk around. 'So, you're looking for someone?'

This conversation needed to end. 'Not anymore, no.' He continued to choose poorly. Deciding to abandon further blunders, he began to walk away.

'I'm sorry.'

He was brought to a stop a few feet behind her. He'd hear her out.

'From a distance, you looked like someone I knew.' She didn't turn to face him; neither did he. 'I thought it was a ghost.'

He understood and could relate. 'Apologies if I startled you.'

'That's okay.'

The wind picked up. It swirled around the park and the sound of rustling leaves surrounded them. She brushed her hair aside and when she looked again, he was gone.

*

'Ah.' Lisara smiled, looking around the alleyway at all the people surrounding her. 'You've cornered me.'

'Lisara,' Calem warned. 'Just come with us, we don't want to hurt you.'

The tip on her sword rested on the ground. She held it out to her side so all here could clearly see it. 'How sweet.' She narrowed her eyes on Calem and whipped her hair from her face with a free hand. 'If you wanted to treat me to dinner, you could have just said so.'

'Just put down the sword.'

A loud clang startled some of those present. Lisara had dropped the blade in front of her.

'Good. Now—'

Before Calem could finish, the sword flipped off the ground and returned to Lisara's hand.

She grinned and shrugged at the blade. 'No... bad boy.'

'Alright, fine! I tried.' He motioned to his people. 'Move in.'

Hesitant but loyal, they all moved closer to Lisara. Not all of them understood the danger. But soon they would.

Quickly and without a moment's pause Lisara defended herself. She deflected blows with her sword and flung them away from her. She cleaved one of their weapons entirely in two and delivered a wide gash to another. She tried her best not to kill them, but the fights until this point had been difficult enough. The scuffle was short and was over quickly, Lisara and a few others left standing. She did not escape entirely unscathed; a few of their attacks got through. Her left arm was bleeding and her right side bruised. Calem's people were not without skill.

Calem fired off a few rounds from his pistol. One of them connected through her pirouettes and pierced her thigh. Through the pain, she managed to wound another attacker and then stood in front of Calem. Her sword sang through the air as he dodged it once. The second swing was too quick for him; he watched the black edge close in on him. But then it stopped. It was stopped.

Athrin stood between them, his hand wrapped firmly around the blade.

Once the surprise had passed, Lisara pulled fiercely to free the sword from his grasp but he held it firmly.

'Athrin!' Calem exclaimed. 'Finally! Quickly, disarm her!'

'Lisara.' Athrin glanced around quickly. He did not have enough information yet; he could not reach a conclusion. 'What is happening?'

Still, she struggled to free the sword, her reaction turned to desperation, then to something close to fear. She swung at his head with her injured arm. He released the blade, not because there was no other option, but because he could see she was hurting herself to free it.

'Go away, Athrin,' she snapped, whipping the sword out to her side and composing herself. Offering him a smile, the usual snark returned. 'I'll drop by later, honey-bear.'

Athrin did not take his eyes off of her. And he remained calm. 'Calem?'

'She attacked the Oracle, Athrin. We're trying to bring her in.' Calem stepped forward, almost to Athrin's side, but not quite. 'Disarm her.'

Athrin could see it in her eyes. She tried to hide it and to most it wouldn't be apparent, her stance and the smirk on her face showed a confidence that was betrayed in her eyes. He could see the panic within her. The realisation that she was alone in this alley.

'Athrin, she—'

'Oh hush, Calem,' she sneered. 'You don't even know what's going on. All you've done is gang up on a cute, innocent little girl.'

'Athrin!'

'I will not follow your orders, Calem,' Athrin said clearly. This he needed to establish before all else.

'That's right, Calem!' She chuckled. 'Athrin is neutral, too good for anyone. Hiding behind his little wall of self-importance.'

'No, you don't understand!' Calem grabbed Athrin's arm. 'She's—'

'Don't tell him!' She swung at them, forcing them apart.

Athrin intervened and kept her attention away from the injured. Carefully, she avoided attacking in such a way that would allow Athrin to grab the blade. When he reached for it, she would pull away and instead swing at him with her fist or a kick. Calem tumbled to the ground, his weapon skid across the ground away from him. Lisara had cornered herself, realising it too late.

'I don't want him to know,' she mumbled.

Slowly, rain started to fall. Steadily at first, then a shower. The drops were ice cold and immediately soaked into their clothing. The blood from those injured began to pool.

Athrin stood before her. Appearing neutral and calm. He would not let them touch her and he would stop her from harming them. That much he had decided already.

'Don't tell him...' she muttered. The rain flattened her hair and tattered clothing. It became more and more apparent just how exhausted she was after all this fighting and running.

Athrin noticed now that her hands were shaking but she gripped the sword in both hands. Blood from her arm dripped to the ground and from the wound on her thigh, running down her leg and pooling around her foot.

'Athrin!' Calem slammed his fist to the ground with a splash. 'It's her! She's the Dragon!'

Lisara cried out, swinging the sword at Athrin without thought or care. He grabbed it. But this time, he called upon that which he had cast away long ago. With it firmly in hand, he pulled Lisara closer and placed his hand over her forehead, his thumb on her temple. It was too quick for her to react, but the dread in her eyes was painfully clear.

CHAPTER XII

CROWDED ISOLATION

He was here again. This area of void. But now he had a form, he was present in a way he had never been before in this place and because of it, he could feel the overwhelming nothingness that surrounded him. And now his suspicions were confirmed. But he was not alone. The huddled form of Lisara was not too far from him; she sat on the ground hugging her knees.

This experience was not entirely strange to him – similar things happened when he took the swords of other Blade Bearers. Yet this was the first time the area was so large, so empty, and so overwhelming.

He approached and called out to her. 'Lisara.' Though she did not respond. He stood a few feet from her before he called again. 'Lisara.'

'She cannot hear you.'

From the void that pressure returned, far more enormous and suffocating than before. The voice came from that void and utterly surrounded him.

Athrin looked around, that perhaps he could make out a shape in the darkness, give this voice a form. 'Show yourself.'

An uncomfortable rumble shook his very being, along with a noise that was eerily close to laughter. When it subsided, the voice re-emerged. 'You should not be here.'

'Yet you have brought me here before.'

Athrin spun around; the voice came from different directions now.

'Not I.' It moved in the same direction as where the figure of Lisara lay.

For a while he had his suspicions, but had nothing to base them upon until now. 'Why?'

But he received no answer.

Athrin reached for her now but the closer he got, the farther away she seemed to drift. He could not close the gap.

The rumbling returned, this time accompanied by a presence and a wave of heat. From the void, the creature appeared. A mighty beast, larger than anything Athrin had ever seen, its eyes bright gold and serpentine. Wide wings unfurled from its body with enough force to knock him from his feet. A slithering tail emerged alongside the beast as it approached Athrin and Lisara. The massive maw opened slightly to reveal multiple rows of razor-sharp fangs. Fire and embers spilled from its mouth with every breath or word. Even though Athrin could not clearly see this beast, wrapped in darkness, one thing was certain; it was an incredible creature and even if only by base primal instincts, he was struck with a tremendous sense of dread.

The massive Dragon dipped its head towards Athrin as if to get a better look at him.

Speechless, Athrin looked over at Lisara. Her form was clutching her head as if in pain. He could see her mouth was open and she was screaming, but no sound escaped her. He summoned every shred of courage he had left and forced words through his throat. 'What are you doing to her?!'

The Dragon only slightly parted its mouth and with seemingly little effort, breathed out a river of fire. The flame engulfed Athrin completely and there would have been nothing left of him had this been real. 'Do not make demands of me, boy.'

Athrin fought through the last of the flames to see Lisara. She still seemed in pain. 'Stop it!' he roared, rushing towards her, but still remained just out of reach.

'Why have you come here, boy?' The Dragon eyed him curiously, as a predator would watch its prey as it struggled needlessly. 'She has done nothing but haunt you.' The Dragon's tail unfurled and swatted Athrin a distance away from Lisara. 'Once, she almost took your life.'

Again, Athrin grabbed for Lisara, desperately trying to help her tormented shape. 'Why are you torturing her?!'

The Dragon seemed disinterested, peering down at them from high above. Its golden eye narrowed on Athrin and observed his every reaction, his every movement. 'Do you intend to rescue her?'

'Leave her alone!'

'Empathy?' The Dragon might have smiled; it could see something in Athrin below the surface. 'Redemption through substitute?' A scoff of flame and embers. 'Hypocrite.'

'Please…' Athrin muttered. The Dragon then glared at him viciously. 'Stop hurting her.'

'You forced your way into her mind and soul, mortal.' The Dragon noticed the change in Athrin as he began to realise what had happened. 'One already made fragile by the sword.'

Athrin recoiled from her, given pause by the words while he deciphered them.

'Fool.' The Dragon turned and receded back into the void, disinterest and disdain melded together in the thick dark veil. 'You are unworthy.'

*

Only a moment had passed. The rain continued, remorseless and unrelenting.

Athrin pulled his hands from Lisara as if he had suddenly been struck by an electric shock. She stood there, motionless, her eyes glazed over. He looked at his hands, contemplating what he had done, what he had caused her.

'Athrin,' Calem called from a short distance away – he and the few of his people that remained approached carefully. 'You did it.'

Athrin heard him but did not respond. He looked at Lisara, her unfocused gaze slowly swept around until she found him, then her vacant blue eyes stayed on him. The blood and rain caused the sword to slip from her fingers and fall to the ground where it disappeared soon after.

'We'll take it from here,' Calem said. He was the only one to get as close as Athrin's side.

After a moment and no response, Calem reached for Lisara. Athrin grabbed his arm, stopping him. 'No' was all he could muster.

'Athrin…' Calem's voice turned to a desperate whisper. 'Don't do this.' He pleaded, freeing his arm with a single tug, 'You know what will happen.'

'No.'

'Please, Athrin. Walk away.'

'I cannot.'

'You must. This will make you an enemy not only of the Girdan but the Order as well. The Sorceress has already been recalled to the city.'

'I am sorry, Calem.'

'Athrin.'

Athrin took a step towards Lisara; her empty eyes followed him. He threw his coat over her shoulders. The extra weight tipped what remained of her strength and she collapsed onto him. He lifted her from the ground into his arms.

'She isn't Amber!' Calem yelled. Athrin did not look at him. 'Trying to save this girl won't bring her back.'

Slowly, Athrin turned and began to walk away.

'Why, Athrin?!'

He didn't stop. He didn't turn back. He didn't care anymore.

*

Rain continued to fall. Not quite a storm, but a shower, enough to sweep the dust and grime from the streets, sufficient for watering the plants, adequate for washing away the blood spilt this day.

The darkened room was surrounded in a veil of cascading water as it ran down the windows, and a gentle pitter-patter against the tin rooves for ambience.

Athrin had the opened box from the bathroom beside him. He dressed Lisara's wounds and ensured her comfort. With a gentle tug he fastened the bandage to her thigh and threw the torn clothing aside. She was still unresponsive and perhaps comatose. Even without his treatment, her wounds were healing miraculously quickly. He assumed the Dragon inside her was to thank for keeping her alive; he had heard the stories of the wielders of that sword before and it seemed a lot of it was true. He took her arm and wiped the dry blood from her skin. The wound had already receded, leaving only a fading scar.

After a moment, he realised he was holding her hand. He ran his thumb over her fingers. Her hands were so much smaller than his and still managed to carry that immense burden. He felt in awe of her. She seemed at peace, lying here in silence. He wondered what was going through her mind and what dreams she may have found herself in. He wondered what she and that Dragon would talk about.

The rain continued to fall, running down the glass and surrounding them in an otherwise surreal atmosphere. He stared out the window, reflecting on the decisions he made to bring him to this point; it still resounded within him. He did not regret it. And he would see it through.

'Are you going to keep that?'

She was looking at him, her expression cautiously neutral. Athrin swapped between her eyes and hand, sharing the sentiment. 'I might.'

A moment passed. Rain beat down on the roof and tapped the glass, all the while they stared at each other. Neither of them knowing what the other was thinking, or what they would do.

'It's a little creepy, Athrin.'

'Are you going to run off if I let go?'

'I might.'

'Then…' His grip tightened slightly. 'Deal with it.'

She pulled her hand from his grasp, looking off to the side to avoid him. 'I have nothing to say to you.'

'Good.' Athrin sat on the sofa beside her. If she wanted to run off, she would need to go through him. 'You talk too much.'

'The hell?'

'Just listen.'

'Suck an egg.'

'What…?'

'Dry up.'

'Lisara.'

'Lick my boots!'

'I am sorry!' he snapped. She did not respond, only fell silent, so he continued. 'I needed to end that fight. I did not know another way.' He thought back to that place, seeing the tremendous form of the Dragon and Lisara huddled in pain. 'I'm sorry.'

Still she did not respond. He looked at her expectantly but she was still turned away.

'You're sorry?' she said finally, still avoiding eye contact. 'You think that's what you should be sorry about?!' Now she whipped her head in his direction, glaring angrily at him, her eyes swelling up. She shoved him from the sofa. He tumbled back a distance but remained on his feet. She leapt after him and grabbed a handful of his shirt. 'I told you to go away!'

She was a full head shorter than he was but that did nothing to deter the fire in her eyes. He had never seen her this angry.

'I left you out of it and you ruined it all!' She grabbed his clothes with both hands and pulled him down to her level where she could yell at him properly. 'Did you think I would crumble in your arms and thank you for saving me?' Her grip tightened. 'All you did was follow your bloated ego and you expect me to feel sorry for you?!'

She paused. Perhaps she was expecting an answer this time but he knew a trap when he saw one. 'I did not.'

With another tug, she hit his head with her own. 'Then why?! They're going to come after you now. They're going to be out for your blood and they're going to burst the little bubble you have carefully crafted around yourself.' She tried to throw him but he clasped her hands and held her grasp in place. 'Why, Athrin? What the hell were you thinking?

'I…'

'That's right! You weren't thinking!' She tugged in the other direction, trying to throw him again, but he held fast. 'I didn't ask you to come after me. I didn't want you to come after me!'

'Well…'

'I left you alone!' She tugged again, her eyes ready to overflow with frustration. 'I tried to. After I saw you weren't what he wanted, I left you alone!'

'Not really…'

She tried again to throw him. This time, she managed to just briefly lift him from his feet but he recovered. 'Why, Athrin?! I left you alone! Why?!'

'I am sick of being alone!'

The tugs and strangling stopped but she still stared at him, still glaring angrily.

'I have been alone for a long time. Wandering through this farce I made, for a reason I had already forgotten. I was sick of it. Sick of being alone in a room full of people.' He kept her gaze, unwavering in his reasoning. 'Same as you.'

'We're not the same.' Her voice betrayed her; it buckled under her words and the tears began to swell.

'No.' He clutched her hands tightly as he felt her grasp slip. 'I selfishly decided that on my own.'

'You did!' She contained what Athrin was sure was a hiccup. 'I was right.'

'Probably.' He guided her hands away from his shirt and neck lest she get a second-wind. 'I came after you because I wanted to.'

'Why?'

He paused. Considered. Then chose poorly. 'My ego?'

Again, she lurched for his neck. He fought back, a brawl he was losing inch by inch. 'Try again.' His leg gave way. In that moment, she took the opportunity and threw him over her shoulder. He slammed to the ground and hit the wall. Quickly, she pinned him in place, kneeling over him. 'Why?'

'Lisara, my arm does not bend that way.'

She tightened her grip in response.

'Amber came after me.' His eyes trailed away from her; he was unsure why. 'And even if, at the time, it seemed like the wrong decision…' He looked at her again, forcing some sort of eye contact regardless of how difficult. 'In the end, I was glad someone did.'

Her glare remained. For quite a while. The feeling in his arm was gone, and he was starting to fear for its survival. Finally, she let him go. His arm returned to him with an uncomfortable pop.

'You shouldn't have,' she mumbled, still kneeling in front of him, her anger replaced by something else – something he wasn't sure he had seen in her before. 'What are you going to do?'

'No idea.'

'Idiot.'

'Why are you giving me a hard time?'

'You dug around in my head.'

'You stabbed me.'

'I'll stab you again!'

He pulled her to the floor. She landed next to him with his hand on her head. '*We* will think of something tomorrow.'

Rain still poured outside. The subtle sounds had been drowned out with all the commotion inside. But now it was allowed to echo again.

Lisara gripped a handful of his clothes, her face buried beneath her hair. They remained here, on the floor and side by side. Athrin patted her head gently.

She mumbled something. He could barely make it out, but there was undeniably a 'honey-bear' in there somewhere.

'Breakfast is on you tomorrow.'

He could feel her nod against his arm. She said nothing, but he noticed quiet sniffling and stifled sobs as her grip tightened. Best to let her have this moment, he thought, and probably best to never bring it up again. Ever.

Chapter XIII

Proportional Purpose

The rain had subsided, leaving only the grey veil of clouds hovering over the city. The sun slowly began to show itself over the horizon, only a peek, the purple glow scattering over the vista.

They had been chatting all night, getting maybe a few hours of sleep. There was a lot to talk about now that the secret was out. Most things still went unanswered nevertheless.

Lisara had showered and pinched one of Athrin's shirts again. They stood out on the balcony staring at the city while the sun shed light on the buildings inch by inch.

'What do you mean?' she asked.

'Exactly that. Where do you come from?'

A smile inched across her lips. 'Well, Athrin, when a mommy and a daddy love each other very much…'

'You know what I mean.'

'Other side of the city.' She pointed in a direction, more than likely the wrong one. 'I thought I told you that already.'

'You did not.' He let out a sigh. Smoke spiralled and folded out in front of him. 'This whole time I thought you were a foreigner.'

'Huh. Why'd you think that?'

He stopped himself from pointing at her hair, instead pulled on his own. 'You know nothing of the city, for one.'

'Well, I didn't go out all that much.'

'Stabbed too many boyfriends?'

She glanced his way, preparing a test. 'Can't remember, there were *so* many.'

A waft of smoke left his mouth through a slow breath. 'Hmm.' He met her gaze. 'I see.'

'Jealous?' She stoked the flame.

Again, he faced the sunrise. 'I wonder if they started a support group.'

The flame died. 'Boring!'

'What is?'

'You!'

'Hm.'

She snatched the cigarette from him. 'I was a prim and proper lady before all of this.' She drew and exhaled a quick breath, passing the cigarette back to Athrin. 'My dad thought me some fragile porcelain doll to be locked away.'

He couldn't picture it. Not even once. But it did begin to explain some things. 'So, a proper princess?'

'Oh, sure, had a butler too.'

'Woah.'

'Right?!'

'Tiara?'

'Several.'

'Mansion?'

'Duh.'

Another slow breath left him, which brought the mood down with it. He decided to ask. 'So, what happened?'

Lisara hummed a short tune while she twirled behind him and leaned on his back, pressing her back to his, and rested her head on his shoulder, then once her tune had ended, she spoke. 'It was a few years ago. Dad was a government official, some or other minister, and one day some maniac broke into the house and cut him down.' The sword appeared over Athrin's shoulder, the blade just in view out the corner of his eye. 'With this.' She paused and slowly started tapping it against his shoulder. 'He didn't kill me though; even warned me to look away. I didn't.'

'I am sorry, Lisara.'

'Don't be.' The tapping stopped, but the sword remained on their shoulders. 'I later found out ol' Dad was a bad dude. Corruption with the Order or something, and I was days away from being sacrificed to some or other cult.'

'How did you end up with it?'

'Not sure.' She chuckled. 'After being passed around from relative to relative and ending up in the country, I found him in a creek.' She tapped him on the side of the head with the blade then let it slip from their shoulders to her side, where she rested the edge lightly on the floor, still firmly in hand. 'You know what happens next.'

'You wait in the rain to stab a complete stranger.'

'Stabbed the hell outta him!'

He tapped another cigarette out from the pack and lit it, slipping the lighter inside the packet and tossing it beside the ashtray. 'It sure has a sick sense of humour.' He leaned back, his head resting on hers. 'Choosing you after all that.'

She pushed back against him. 'I chose him. I didn't have to.'

'I am sure it seemed that way.'

'A lot of people think that, Athrin. A lot of them are wrong.'

He stood straight, resisting her force. 'You do not think it forced you into this situation?'

'Did he force you?'

Athrin stared at the cloud of smoke from his breath, thinking on her words and where they may have come from, thinking if there was any truth to it. He had made his own decisions, he thought. 'No.' Another breath in and out, the swirling cloud wrapped around the view in front of him. 'Did it make you attack me?'

She rolled on his back to lean on him with her side, her head still resting on his shoulder. 'No. He was mad at me after that.'

He felt a tap on his shoulder, he reached over and handed her the cigarette. She grasped his hand and slowly took it from him.

'I wanted to kill whoever he chose. When I saw what was in you, I knew he'd pick you.' A waft of smoke floated past Athrin and dissipated into the distance. She handed it back to him. 'I wasn't ready for that.'

'Because?'

She poked his ribs making him flinch and nearly slip from his handhold. 'Enough about me.'

That wasn't good enough; he wanted to know. He had heard stories of the Dragon and what happened to those it possessed. None of them ended well. He needed to know. 'Lisara, tell me why.'

She grabbed a handful of his side, shirt and flesh. 'I've spilt enough of the beans.'

Through gritted teeth, he fought the pain. 'This is important.'

'Aren't you supposed to be clever enough to piece it together on your own?'

'I am under duress at the moment...'

The grip tightened. Then she released him, and he was allowed to breathe easy again, for a moment. 'I didn't want to be alone again.'

Sadly simple. And not what he was expecting. Usually, the cost was higher.

'I'm sorry, Athrin.'

He peeked over his shoulder. Only the top of her head was visible, her hair splayed across his back.

'I didn't mean to hurt you.'

There were a fair few instances of physical harm inflicted by her that came to mind. He wondered which.

'Back then...'

Their first meeting.

'I'm sorry.' She clutched his side again, missing his flesh this time. Mostly.

Athrin grumbled some, mulling over the words in his mind as he ground them into a reply. 'I will forgive you, if you make it up to me...' he began, as he crushed the cigarette into the ashtray. His thoughts cycling between past and present, he wanted to do something. This felt right. 'By not running off.'

He didn't care about before, a wound in battle never meant anything to him. These last few years had left him hollow, a gap he could never seem to fill no matter what he did. But now, in these moments, he felt more complete. Civility? Perhaps that wasn't what the promise meant after all. He looked from her and out at the city – vast and colourful as it was, it filled him with an abstract uneasiness. 'That way, neither of us will be alone.'

They shared a time of silence. It passed with the sun sweeping over them, emerging from behind the buildings and soaring over the horizon. Athrin capped his eyes from the bright light to better see the city. Perhaps it wasn't so bad after all.

A snickering started behind him, which steadily grew into laughter. 'What?' he inquired.

'Oh, Athrin.' She stumbled over her laughter. 'That was so very cheesy.'

He snapped to the city, grumbling under his breath.

She rolled over to bury her face in his back, stifling the chuckles. 'You really are something.'

More grumbling.

The chuckling passed. 'But…'

A few more grumbles.

She smiled. 'I like that idea.'

*

This was wrong. Athrin remembered going to sleep. He knew exactly where and when but he was in a different place now. This place was unfamiliar to him and just as ethereal.

Around him, a veil of white light, before him far in the distance, he could make out a pond. In the centre of this pond was a white tree and what appeared to be two people. One was a woman dressed in a white dress, melding her with the surroundings and made her seem at one with this place. Beside her was another woman, perhaps familiar. The two of them seemed to be speaking with one another, like old friends.

Then the woman in white turned abruptly to Athrin; she pointed at him. With a sudden jerk, Athrin felt as if his very being was being ripped apart. A moment later he found himself standing before the two of them. He looked back from where he had come, realising he had traversed that distance in an instant.

'It is because he touched the tree,' the woman in white went on to say.

Athrin turned to her, clad in pure white. She exuded elegance, not merely moving but gliding with each motion. She was difficult to look at, her radiance and presence blinding in the light.

'Do you think he knows where it is?' the other woman asked.

Either from shock of the transition or merely as a result of this place, Athrin found it difficult to move, his mind in a fugue state and barely holding on to any semblance of lucidity.

'He certainly knows of it.' The woman in white focused her attention on their conversation; both of them paid him little heed, he was merely present. 'But I cannot speak to his intentions.'

'Who...' Athrin made to speak but words failed him. They glanced at him briefly, curious, but then returned to their conversation.

'Take heed, for he knows you are near,' the woman in white said to the other, offering her a comforting hand on her shoulder. 'He will have prepared for you.'

'Why...' Athrin fought through the haze, his gaze cycling in and out of focus.

'This one is resilient,' the other said to the woman in white, taking a step closer to Athrin. 'Oh. I recognise him.'

*

The city was buzzing with excitement. The parade day was drawing nearer and the people prepared for this important day. Just below the surface, in the shadows of the norm, was equal excitement but coloured with dread and anxiety. Eyes were open, ears were listening, the search for the Dragon continued.

'This way, Athrin!' Lisara laughed, leaping over the railing and vanishing down the alley.

With equal speed, Athrin followed, clearing the railing in a single bound. He remained only a few feet behind her. And he was impressed that he could still keep pace. Behind them, fading into the distance, were Calem's scouts. They had been spotted again today and were aiming to lose them in the city. It had been three days of this, Athrin chasing after Lisara while she was pursued. She seemed to enjoy it, laughing merrily as she sprinted through the alleyways with an almost unnatural speed and dexterity.

Eventually he caught up to her. She waited in an alley, checking the corners and leaning out to see if anyone was still following. She was not, in the least bit, out of breath, though Athrin was nearing his limit.

'Like I...' He paused to catch his breath. 'Like I said, we should have waited for dark.'

'Poopy.' She approached him. 'Where's the fun in that?'

'Fun, huh?' He leaned against the wall, recovering the rest of his breath.

'You okay?'

'All good. It has been a while.'

She snickered at him. 'It's all those 'bacco sticks.' She grabbed his hand and pulled him along. 'Come on.'

Answering with a groan, he let her lead him. 'No more close calls, please, Lisara.'

'Dude, stop whining. Aren't you a man?'

'You wound me, miss.'

'Pipe down, thesaurus.'

They walked through the city, blending in with the crowds. Lisara pulled Athrin by hand to all the sights that caught her eye; some had her in awe while others were simply confusing. Like the fountain skipping water over a metal cube. It was clear to him that perhaps she had always wanted to see the city, but for whatever reason she was unable to.

A gaggle of school children herded by some adults passed them by. Lisara watched them with interest and amusement. Athrin noticed it, taken aback by how different it was to see her wearing an earnest smile instead of a mischievous one.

They passed by some stores, one of which she encouraged Athrin to purchase something for her. Immediately she fit the hairpin just above her ear, glowing as she admired it intently in the mirror.

'What do you say?' Athrin mumbled while he finished with the store clerk.

'Uh…' She looked around the store, in search of an exit, then shot out the door calling after him. 'Come, Clouse, bring the luggage.'

The store clerk offered her sympathies in the form of a gentle smile, then Athrin hurried off after Lisara lest she run off with something from another store. Or worse, attract more attention.

'I am not buying shoes,' Athrin growled while she pulled him into another store, the smell of brand new, overly expensive, merchandise near poison to him but no doubt ambrosia to Lisara.

A man in flamboyant suit-like attire approached them as they entered, a wide grin on his face. 'What can I get for the lovely couple?'

'Couple?!' they both yelled together. The entire store came to a standstill and peered around for signs of trouble. Lisara pointed at Athrin with such ferocity there was an indent in his cheek. 'He wishes!'

'I do not.'

'Boots! Heels! Stat!' She abandoned Athrin and followed the frolicking velvet-shaped man towards possible treasure.

Athrin, however, was left in the middle of all the onlookers. He could almost taste the thick pity and sprinkles of disdain in the air. Seizing the opportunity to retreat, he left the store, shooting a glare at a few of the more tenacious observers on his way out.

*

Athrin finished a cigarette and tossed the remains into the metal drum near him. He peered over to the store again. It had been some time but he knew it could still take longer. He had forgotten this feeling. It was different, of course it was, but he didn't mind that. A sliver of a smile crept across his default frown. Perhaps it wasn't all that bad. With a single sweep, he cast his gaze on the city and the people before him, and he could not remember the last time when he could honestly say he did not despise being here. Maybe, just maybe, this was it.

'Honey-bear!'

Maybe not.

Lisara tossed a bag at him – he caught it just in time, then she stood before him and twirled for show. 'What do you think?'

This was a test. He had prepared for moments such as these. But those training courses were so long ago, and he never did score highly. Quickly, he examined her clothes; they were the same. Probably. The bag in his hands. The shop. 'Shoes,' he said cautiously.

She admired them, tugging on the leg of her pants to get a better look. 'Fancy, right?'

Success.

He noticed them, slender boots with a heel. She was a little taller as a result. Then, something occurred to him. His grip tightened on the bag. 'Did you steal them?'

She glared at him. 'You're right. We may need to run.' With a shove, she separated him from the wall and they started walking. 'No, you idiot. I paid for them.'

'You?' He looked at the bag, then at the shop, then finally at her. 'With money?'

She winked at him, with an almost audible twinkle. 'Daddy didn't raise a fool, yo.'

A rather sinking feeling swelled up inside of him, one which he could only describe as having the word 'sucker' scribbled on his forehead. 'This whole time...?'

'Don't feel too bad.' She smiled with a 'teehee' and tossed him a rather familiar-looking wallet. 'You can keep the change.'

'This is mine...'

'Honey-bear!' she called, now from nearly a street away. She stood provocatively in her new boots, with one finger on her bottom lip, her long blonde hair flowing in the gentle breeze. Onlookers beware. 'Treat me to lunch?'

*

Athrin trudged with a pair of boots in one hand, a bag in the other, and a weight on his back growing heavier and heavier with every movement or word.

'Mush!' Lisara commanded, leaning on his head.

'I will drop you.'

'But my footsies are sore, Athrin!'

'I told you not to wear them.' He sneered at the footwear in his hand, needing to fight the urge to toss them a distance. 'You need to break them in first.'

She leaned closer to his ear, blocking out the glare from the sunset. 'Will you wear them for me?'

An audible chuckle burst from him, taking both of them by surprise. 'Not a chance.' He turned a sharp corner, causing her to nearly lose balance. 'I would sooner light them on fire and bury them in a ditch.'

'Athrin!' she scolded, slapping his head. 'Those were a gift!'

He managed to stifle the resulting chuckle. 'The hairpin was a gift. These are a felony.'

Her fingers threaded through her hair until they found the pin, she felt it lightly and ran her finger over the silver decoration. 'I know…'

'Oh?' He trotted across the street just as the light turned orange. 'Rendered speechless, could it be?'

A quick flick to his ear. 'If you're going to make me feel guilty about it, maybe you should light them on fire.'

'Can I?!'

'Please don't…' She grabbed a handful of his hair, ready to yank in protest. 'And don't sound so excited about it!'

'I will make sure they do not suffer.'

'Don't!' With a tug, she pulled his ear closer. 'I'll make it up to you.'

'Go on.'

She smiled and with a breathy whisper, aimed to take years off Athrin's life. 'Tonight… under the covers…'

With a jerk left and right, he tried to throw her off his back like a bucking horse but she held tightly around his neck, laughing at his reaction.

The scuffle ended and the walk continued. 'You're such a softie, Athrin.'

He growled and grumbled his way down the rest of the path.

She clutched the back of his collar between her fingers and rested her head on his, rosy cheeks and a gentle smile hidden where he couldn't see.

Chapter XIV

Light That Burns

'Stay on your side.' Lisara pushed Athrin away with her shoulder while still juggling pan and spatula.

Athrin resisted, pushing back but still needing to stretch over her to reach his pan and prevent the bacon and sausages from burning. 'I am. You are invading mine.'

She threw another pinch of salt over the omelette. 'Saboteur! Be gone!'

'It is burning on its own and will not need my help.' He watched her throw another pinch of salt. 'Enough with the salt!'

After some pokes, jabs and a spatula-slap, they had somehow switched sides. Determination in her eyes, Lisara glared at Athrin's pan, searching for some way to interfere. His technique was infuriatingly faultless. 'Athrin, quick, your couch is on fire!'

'At least you will be warm tonight,' he mumbled, unperturbed. This was hardly her first attempt.

She stuck her tongue out at him but he probably didn't notice.

Other than the quiet sizzling and sporadic outcries, it was quiet tonight. The star-speckled sky was clear and bright; it would be easy to see far tonight. Athrin, battle-scarred and weary from the great food war, focused on recovering the bacon in front of him from the edge of charred. Out of the corner of his eye, he snuck a look at Lisara's pan. It wasn't burnt. Yet. He looked at her, a pout but also determination in her expression, even though she denied it he could tell she had never done anything like this before. She seemed to be enjoying it. He might have as well.

'Uh-oh. Athrin…' she began. 'The oven mitt is on fire.'

'Ah, that is too bad. I liked that one.'

'Athrin… it is actually on fire.'

It was.

*

An ordeal later and finally they had sat down to eat. Athrin stared at the plate for the longest time, wondering if it was all worth it. He was an oven mitt down, had probably lost a pan, two spatulas had been disfigured, all of the salt was somehow gone, and he was sure a few years had been shaved off his lifespan. But then he looked at Lisara. She was in her own little world, happily munching and laughing at him. He felt it within himself. Yes, it was worth losing a spatula or two.

'Might be a little too much salt.'

Perhaps he'd draw the line at two.

'The bacon isn't too bad.' She smiled at him. 'Guess you didn't destroy it after all.'

'Despite your efforts, yes, I believe it came out alright.' He began carving his plate. 'And the omelette is not terrible.'

'Excuse you.' She aimed her fork at him menacingly. 'I'll have you know a lot of effort went into it.'

'And salt.'

'Love, Athrin, love.'

'Is that what that is…' He poked the omelette playfully. 'Lumpier than I thought.'

A fork flew across the room and imbedded into the sofa right beside Athrin, narrowly missing a vital point.

When the surprise passed, he checked the damage. 'Oi!'

She growled at him. Like a predator would its prey, to remind it of how much smaller it was. With an outstretched hand, she growled at him again. He tossed his fork to her, skilfully snatching it out the air she continued with her plate. And now he was left, forkless.

With a tug, he freed the make-shift weapon and wiped it down on a napkin.

'Don't...' She glared at him.

The polishing continued. 'What?'

'Just don't.'

'What?'

'Don't use it.'

'I am cleaning it; it will be fine.'

She readied her new weapon, prepared to add another few holes to the sofa. Or to Athrin.

'Fine.' He stood and tossed the fork into the sink, grabbing a clean one from the dish rack. He could not understand what the fuss was about; perhaps she knew something he did not. He sat down again. 'It is just a fork.'

She growled at him some more, mopping up the last of the omelette on her plate, her cheeks flushed. 'And stop laughing.'

'I am not.'

'Not you, stupid.' She pointed towards the window with her toe. 'Him.'

Athrin did not need to look around the room to know that they were alone. It only took a moment for him to draw an assumption. 'Has it been here this whole time?'

'It?'

'The Dragon.'

'Him, Athrin. Not *it*.'

She sounded annoyed, through familiarisation or personification it seemed she had a different opinion on just what, or who, the Dragon was. Athrin could not deny that he was interested in it. He had only heard the stories. 'Has he been here this whole time?' he corrected himself.

'No,' she began, sliding her empty plate across the table, knife and fork clanking from the half-spin as it settled. 'It's quite rare, he doesn't engage much. He must be hungry.'

'Quite a small room to accommodate that large of a being.' He chose his words carefully.

Her eyebrow raised slightly in response, then straightened. 'Ah. He can change his appearance. You see him as…?'

'A dragon.' Athrin filled the gap. 'A very large dragon.'

'Oooo.' She smiled, leaning forward a little to better see his reactions from her perch. 'I saw it once or twice. Scary, right?'

He thought back to that sight, that moment, the towering creature's very presence engulfed him so utterly and completely.

'Scary?' Athrin repeated. He chewed on bacon and eggs for a while. 'Daunting' was the word he'd choose. His mind wandered during the silence, he thought still on his meeting with the Dragon, then another question came to him, one he wasn't sure he wanted to ask but did anyway. 'Does he torment you?' Her huddled form had come to mind.

'No.' Her response was stern and without pause. Then her expression softened. She lifted her feet from the floor and hugged her knees, still looking straight at Athrin. 'He was the first to give a shit about me.' Her stare remained neutral, assessing and sharing. 'He was the first to ask me what *I* wanted to do.' Now she paused and looked to a corner of the room. 'Instead of what I should do.'

Athrin mopped the last of his plate and slid it over hers, trying his best to quieten the jingling and rolling metal. He wanted to say more, to explain what he was thinking and what made him ask these things. But he was never good with conversations and forming what he intends into words. Besides, Lisara beat him to it.

'A lot of people think he's some monster.' She was looking at him again, intensely, but it did not seem to be directed at him per se. 'I heard them talking, while they were hunting me like an animal. They think he's some heartless ass-bucket.'

Two heads in the room may have turned. But Athrin was sure it was only his.

'It's not true, Athrin!' she yelled, slamming her fist to the sofa with an unsatisfying 'poof'. 'He didn't want any of this to happen.'

Athrin said nothing. He would listen.

'Those people out there trying to kill us, they're fools. They should be working with us.' Her grip seemed to tighten around her legs and her head slowly crept behind her knees. '… Or they should just leave us alone.'

For a time, Athrin mulled over what she had said. The stories he had heard and the lessons he was taught about and around the Dragon through all of his years, however limited, were put in doubt after only the past week. To be fair, he had never conformed to the Dragon hunt. Present or past.

'Lisara,' he began. Her eyes emerged from cover. 'Then, what does he want?'

'I don't know.' She looked away again, preparing for the inevitable questions she had always received. The interrogations and doubt.

'Okay.'

'… Huh?'

He brought her pause. Still their eyes locked. 'I believe you.'

She had her reasons. Her aim. He knew this. That much at least. The Dragon, for good or ill, always had a goal for each one that carried the burden. She didn't have to tell him, he didn't need to know. He decided to do what he could anyway. Was it for her? For himself? To prove something to another? He didn't know. He didn't care.

It may have been a glare, her furled brow and scrunched nose supported the theory, but she found herself staring at him. And almost certainly she had underestimated him. 'Doesn't take much to convince you anymore.'

'Would you rather I grabbed a torch and a pitchfork then chased you down the street?'

She was standing in front of him now. He wasn't sure when she had moved. 'You'd chase me, would you?'

'If the need arose.'

Lisara leaned forward, putting her hand on his knee, bringing their eyes but inches apart. 'You're not falling in love with me, are you, Athrin?'

'I think…' He paused, keeping eye contact. 'I am incapable.'

Slowly Lisara began to close the gap until her lips very nearly met his. She stared at him, waiting for some kind of reaction, but she could not see anything. 'That's good then.' She pushed away from him with a shove against his chest, still watching him as a smile slowly crept across her lips. 'You missed your chance.'

'To be stabbed again?' Athrin stood and grabbed the dishes, making his way to the sink. 'Pass.'

'Maybe I should stab you again.' She followed him across the room, opening the faucet pre-emptively. 'The way you go on about it, I think you liked it.'

'Loved it.' He dropped the dishes in the sink and soaked the sponge. 'Loss of blood, hazy vision, incredible pain. A regular Friday night.'

She leaned over the counter, watching his hands while he scrubbed the dishes and utensils. 'You missed a spot.'

'I just started.'

'And already you've ruined it.'

His hands stopped. He offered her the sponge. 'If you wanted to do it, you only have to ask.'

She snatched the sponge and shoved him out the way. 'Watch and learn, dude.'

*

This was a dream. It had to be.

A large room. Darkened save for the dim light seeping through the overcast clouds and shining through the broken and ruined ceiling. Once this place may have been a fantastic throne room, the king and his advisors would have been spread around the throne which still stood, decrepit, at the back of the hall.

'Who are you?!' a creature, who had taken the ruined stronghold for itself and its minions, roared angrily. The creature's voice was strong and loud. It echoed clearly within the entire structure, its words speckled with grunts, growls and snarls.

A lone man emerged from the shadows leading up to the entrance to the hall; behind him, he dragged the carcass of a similar creature as the one before him, albeit smaller in stature. He tossed the cadaver between the two of them and faced the creature confidently. 'A demon hunter,' he said at last.

Snarls and growling erupted from the creature, akin to laughter. It stood tall and menacingly. 'Ridiculous.' It put one foot forward, the thump echoed off the walls. 'You are but a human.'

Around them the floor was riddled with skeletons and scattered bones, both old and new, it was clear this place had been a battlefield. And a conquest.

The man took his sword into his main hand and walked forward, clear in his intentions.

'To your death then,' the creature spat. When it opened its hand, a gigantic, crudely crafted greatsword crashed through the debris and met its grasp. 'You have done well to sneak past my guards, human,' it snarled aggressively. 'But now you will know pain like no other.'

'I killed your minions,' the man said simply, still on the approach. 'The rest ran like rats.'

The creature roared in fury and began running for him, the greatsword dragging sparks on the ground behind it. As they came in range of one another, the creature swung the sword with all the might it had. The next moment it stood alone; the human had vanished. Frantically, it searched for him and found him standing a few feet behind it. Beside the man was the creature's sword embedded into the ground, its arm still attached to the grip.

'The arrogant ones are all the same,' the man began. The black blood ran down the length of his sword.

The creature watched him, seemingly unperturbed by the loss of a limb but instead cautious of this man.

The man continued. 'They cannot fathom that there is something stronger than they are.'

Angered once again, the creature ran for him, teeth bare.

'There is always someone stronger.'

In a quick movement, the man slashed across the creature's front. In the moment opened by the attack, he grabbed its head and using the momentum of its sprint, whipped its body off the ground. Its head remained in his hand, separated from the neck after a quick slash from his sword. The creature's body tumbled to a halt a distance away, a trail of thick black blood marking its course.

The man threw the head to the side and then wiped his sword clean on the creature's padded armour. With a quick snap, he sheathed the sword at his side. After a moment he looked around the room. He knew this place. He had been here before. Though now it was almost entirely unrecognisable. 'I am coming for you.' His gaze narrowed on the crude banner impaled into the remains of the throne. 'Dragon.'

*

Athrin woke from a bizarre dream to the sound of knocking. Someone was at the door. He struggled to free himself from the sheets, realising too that Lisara had snuck into the bed again and was lying over his side.

Another few knocks.

He wrenched from her grasp and pulled a jacket over his shoulders as he made his way to the entrance. After a quick tug on the collar, he opened the door.

'Ah, Athrin, is it?'

It took him a moment to focus his eyes and be sure he was not still dreaming. This was not good.

'Did I wake you?'

He was not imagining it. It was her. The woman he met briefly at the tree, both in reality and vision, and he knew what this meant.

'You're a hard man to find,' she said lightly, taking a moment to glance at the building again. 'I've seen people suppress their signature before, but to do it for an entire building is... impressive.'

Too soon. He knew they would find him eventually but he had taken steps to delay it for at least another few days.

'I didn't recognise you at first,' she continued, remaining calm and sociable. 'Back at the park the other day.' With a thumb, she gestured behind her. 'I haven't been with the Order for quite a while.'

Athrin gripped the door tightly; he assessed the situation and considered the options. There might still be a way out of this.

'Neither have you, apparently.' She smiled, sliding stray hairs behind her ear. 'Do you remember me?'

He nodded slowly. 'I do.' He knew more of her indirectly, by reputation and account. 'Kasari. The Sorceress.'

'Awesome. That makes this easier.' She still smiled, but the importance was in her eyes. She kept locked onto him, monitoring his every movement and response. And then, the question came. 'Is she here?'

There it was, the slim chance to avoid confrontation. But then, as if right on que, a quiet rustling seeped from the other room. 'Honeybear...' An awkward pause. 'Is that room service?' Impeccable.

Kasari noticed his sigh and almost chuckled. 'Don't worry, I knew she was here. Felt it as soon as you opened the door.'

Plan B. Athrin straightened himself and put one hand on the door frame to close any gap inside. 'You should leave.'

'You know I can't do that.'

'Yet you should anyway.'

'Let me take her, Athrin.' He noticed her left foot turn a few degrees as she spoke; she had readied her footing. 'I am not with the Order or the Girdan, I work with Oracle Alari.'

Slowly Athrin slid one foot a few inches back. His left hand on the door moved up slightly. It did not go unnoticed.

'You should leave,' he said again.

'She has killed people, Athrin. I can't just let it go.' Her right hand opened at her side and a strange light twinkled in her palm. 'You think you're the first person she has visited? You think you're the first person she has taken advantage of?'

That he did not know. He hadn't considered it. But it did not matter. 'Please. Leave.'

'She is dangerous, Athrin.' Still Kasari spoke gently, kindly. It seemed her intent was not aggression. 'You should know, letting the Dragon run rampant is a terrible idea. Do you remember what happened last time he was in the city?'

Athrin's grip tightened. His breath skipped for but a moment. But he very quickly set himself again.

'Of course you do,' she continued calmly, lightly assuring him as she moved towards an obviously contentious exchange. 'I asked around about you. And then it made sense.'

Now Athrin struggled to keep his breathing under control, but he still had the better of it. 'Leave.'

'And yet you protect her and the Dragon?'

Sounds of slow bare feet dragged behind him, with but a quick glance he knew Lisara had just emerged from the bedroom, still rubbing the sleep from her eyes. 'Athrin,' she mumbled, poking her finger through a hole in the shirt she wore. 'Your shirt has a hole in it.'

Kasari looked at Lisara now; her demeanour immediately changed as if she was staring down a mortal enemy. Steeling herself, she then turned to Athrin again. 'Even after all they put you through?'

Chapter XV

Cognisant Ambiguity

'Wait, what?'

'Yeah, yeah. She came back a week ago.'

He stroked the stubble on his chin as if it was a larger, more luscious beard. 'Wait… what?'

'What part did you not get?'

'The part where you know what you're talking about.' He topped off the glass and slid it across the bar to his partner. "Coz you never do.'

'Ask Zieg then, you filthy troglodyte.' He grabbed the glass, nearly missing it as it almost slid off the edge.

'Why would Zieg know?'

'They go way back, man.'

'Way back, like…' He showed his hand and crossed two fingers. 'Way back?'

'How would I know?!' He took a swig and slammed the glass on the bar, quickly making sure he didn't damage either. 'You ask him!'

He snorted loudly and stored the bottle. 'As if. Dude will snap my neck.' He took enough time to line it up perfectly and make as though no one had touched it. 'I think you're just full of it.'

'Full of whiskey!' They clinked their glasses together and both emptied them with a long swig.

'We're clear, yeah?'

'Crystal.'

A voice thundered through the room. The bottles and glasses behind the bar rattled. 'Benny, Davey! Get your arses over here.'

'He's back…'

'See! I told you. She must be back!'

The voice resounded again, a little more serious this time. 'You lads better replace that bottle.'

Collectively they slid their glasses into the sink, gently enough to not damage them. Naturally.

'I hate you.'

'Love you too, bro.'

*

Like a bolt of lightning, Lisara leapt over Athrin, the sword forming in her grasp as she passed over his shoulder and connected with Kasari. The two of them tumbled over the railing, both landing squarely on the ground in the yard. Kasari pulled a sword out of thin air, a long slender blade almost blinding in the light with its silver glow, a stark contrast to the black blade in Lisara's hands. Not a moment passed before the two swords connected, black and silver, the two glared at each other across the steel. The battle ensued.

Athrin watched from above, both impressed and surprised by their speed and skill, while Kasari seemed to be the more experienced fighter. Lisara did not seem to be struggling to keep up with her. That overwhelming strength could not be ignored.

This was hardly the ideal outcome, but one that Athrin had seen coming. Plan C. As quickly as he could, he darted inside his home, grabbing a few select items and stuffing them inside his bag. He would have to abandon his home now. This place he had managed to keep hidden for so long. Though hardly a new concept to him, he had never been in one place for too long. This place was not without worth.

He was in the bedroom. Through the walls he could still make out the clashing of steel and yells of the fight. But here there was something else that took precedence. The picture. For a brief moment he considered leaving it, entirely abandoning this place and its memories, but he could not entertain that thought for long. He grabbed the frame and pulled the photo through the back, putting it neatly in his pocket. Safely. Then he opened the drawer right below the frame and removed a small wrapped pouch, something glittering inside. Something red.

A cry returned him to the present. Quickly he raced from the apartment and leapt over the balcony to the yard below.

Kasari stood over Lisara; their swords crossed but she had managed to inch past the black blade's defences and pierce Lisara's shoulder. Kasari grabbed Lisara's wrist and pulled her sword arm away. A subtle glow came from her eyes and her sword shared it. 'You didn't pick a good enough fighter this time.' She growled at a spectre.

Lisara winced as her arm was twisted. The sword fell from her grasp and Kasari seemed poised to sever her arm.

As the blade came down, Athrin had reached them. He stopped the silver blade just as it reached Lisara's arm. He pulled her from Kasari's grasp and forced himself between them, still clutching the silver sword.

Though surprised, Kasari remained calm. 'Don't do this, Athrin.'

Blood squeezed through his grip and trickled to the ground. 'I will not let you take her.'

'It is the only way to stop him.' She twisted and pulled, trying to free the blade. But with one hand to help Lisara, Athrin struggled to keep his grip. A thicker stream of blood ran down the blade. 'It is the only way to free her.'

'By killing her?'

'The moment she made the deal her fate was sealed.' She grabbed for Athrin's arm and gripped it tightly, perhaps to avoid hurting him further. 'She is dead either way.'

'You do not know that.'

'I do!'

He could see it. For a moment, her calm demeanour had slipped away and revealed something else, though she quickly corrected it.

She glared at him, more determination in her eyes than anything else. 'If you cannot show me another way, do not brand me the monster.'

Those words. He had heard them before.

Athrin scoffed. Something welled up from within him. Anger, perhaps. Disappointment, maybe. There was once someone who used those words, lived by them, hid behind them and died by them. She did not understand the meaning, could not fathom the conviction and did not deserve them.

'There is always another way!' Athrin shouted angrily, pulling free from Kasari's grasp and tugging on the sword to bring her closer, close enough to see the truth in her eyes. 'Those words do not excuse cowardice,' he sneered.

Lisara stirred at his side, clutching his arm as she stumbled to her feet.

'Those are not your words,' Athrin continued calmly again. He had her full attention, the surprise clear in her eyes. 'And you will not dishonour him.'

With his arm free, Athrin reached out for Kasari and placed his hand over her forehead, his thumb on her temple. Suddenly she was aware of what was happening; she realised what Athrin was and what he was about to do. And she was too late to stop it.

*

He was in a hallway. The walls lined with doors and numbers. This was an apartment block, not unlike his, only on the fancier side of town. He stood in front of a door already. It was a little different from the others, smarter wood, varnished, as if out of all the others this one was somehow special. He could hear something within. A voice.

Steadily he grasped the door handle and made his way inside.

The apartment was smart, well-kept and decorated. On the far end, by the window, was a living room of three sofas and a coffee table between them. Closer to him, on the right wall, was a stand adorned with picture frames and a ceremonial stand with swords. Perhaps a memorial of some sort.

He heard the voice again. A woman humming.

To his left was an opening without a door leading to the kitchen. The humming grew louder as he approached. In the kitchen, he found Kasari. Her hair loose and long enough to pass her shoulder. She stood over the stove and stirred a pot as the humming continued.

She turned in his direction. Athrin paused but she seemed unable to see him, instead making her way to the panty.

'Spices, spices,' she muttered, jogging to the shelves and digging through the assorted bottles and shakers.

Athrin noticed how different she seemed. Perhaps a lot of people might gloss over it. But he could tell. She was different.

She cradled the wooden spoon on the pot and began gathering her hair behind her head to tie a ponytail.

Suddenly, another presence emerged out of thin air. The form approached her, almost menacingly, as if about to attack her. Athrin stepped forward to intervene, but then, 'Oooo, sporty Kassie!' A man grabbed her from behind, lifting her off the ground and twirling while she struggled to tie her hair.

'Myan!' she snapped, tying the band and pressing on his head with her elbow. 'Put me down!'

'I found this!' His words were a little slurred from the elbow pressed to his face, but he held firmly. 'Finder's keepers.'

'You can't "keep" me, you idiot!' She managed to squirm enough and turn to be able to fight him off with both hands.

'Ooh, I beg to differ.'

They stumbled around the room laughing, Myan managed to keep her in his grasp no matter how much she struggled. Even though she kicked and shoved, she looked happy.

Now, Athrin was sure. He understood this, related even, but he was not expecting to see him.

'Myan, the stew!' she cried, reaching for the pot, but was still just out of reach and securely restrained.

'Stew?' He stopped swaying her back and forth, following her outstretched arm to the stove. 'Beef?'

'It'll be charcoal if you don't let me get back to it!'

'That doesn't sound very nice.'

'Myan.'

'I mean, I'll probably eat it anyway, not making comments about your cooking or anything.'

'Myan.'

'Though, when you're not looking, I might chuck it out the window. Not that I've done that before...'

'Myan!'

'Ugh, fine.' He released her from the vice and followed her closely as she sped back to the stove, fiddled with the dials, and began furiously stirring the bubbling pot.

'Stir this, I need to check on the rice.' She turned to him, offering the wooden spoon.

'I need to cook now too?!'

She smacked his cheek with the spoon and offered it again, accompanied this time by a growl.

'I had a dream like this once...' He took the spoon and stared curiously at the pot. 'Different cheek though.'

She skipped a few steps to the counter close by and checked the rice cooker. 'Just stir the pot, stupid.'

They stood here, for a time. Every now and then Kasari would glance over at Myan, her cheeks somewhat flushed, and she would stare at him. Obliviously, he would scratch something from the spoon or almost burn his finger and she would see it. And she would miss it.

Right before Athrin's eyes, the scene dissolved, like a sheet of paper burning in a violent flame. It was replaced with a darkened room, perhaps a bedroom.

Athrin looked around the new surroundings. A thin sliver of moonlight passed through a crack in the curtains but did little to offer light to the room.

Eventually, he could hear her before he saw her. Kasari was slumped over the bed, her knees on the floor. She was sobbing quietly. Muttering things Athrin could not hear. He didn't want to. Such was an invasion, more so than what he had seen already. But his feet moved on their own. As he drew nearer, the whispers became clear.

'I'm sorry.' She wept, unable to stop the tears streaming from her eyes. 'Myan... I'm sorry.'

Athrin was frozen. He connected the dots, drew some lines in his mind to try and make sense of what he knew and what he was seeing.

But then he realised Kasari was looking at him. She had stood up from the bed and glared at him furiously. Surprisingly enough, she could see him now. With bare feet, she stomped across the floor towards him and reeled her arm back. 'Get out!'

*

The city bustled with excitement as the people cheered and laughed. The day had come. Most streets were closed off today, for the event, deserted and mostly unmonitored. Some relied on this.

In the city square, where most of the people and cheering gravitated to, stood a podium decorated with national colours. It stood waiting. Waiting for the guest to arrive.

*

Kasari broke free from Athrin's grasp. Her fist had connected with him and they stumbled away from each other. Athrin was surprised. That had never happened before.

She seemed to be disoriented, trying desperately to find her footing. Whatever she was able to do was clearly having an effect on her.

Athrin grabbed Lisara's arm. She seemed to have recovered in this time, but remained confused about what had transpired. 'We need to go.' He grabbed his bag and ran with Lisara, away from Kasari. Away from his home.

They ran through the streets, took routes down alleyways, hopped over fences, crossed a train track, and when they could not run anymore, they stopped. Wounded and exhausted in this alley.

Athrin slid to the ground, leaning on the wall for support, and tossed his bag to the side. Lisara emerged a moment later, wearing more than a torn shirt. She stood in front of him, in hesitant silence.

He tightened the rag he had wrapped around his hand then looked up at her. 'Here.' He stretched his hand out to her and she helped him to his feet. 'Let me check your shoulder.'

'It's fine.'

Ignoring her, he felt the spot where he thought there would be a wound. But there was nothing. He took her arm and checked for other injuries, so far finding nothing. As expected. Her burden had some benefits.

She stood in place, her head lowered, letting him check her arm and avoided eye contact whenever it came close.

Her silence and mood did not go unnoticed. Once he finished with her arm, he would humour her. 'What is wrong?'

'What do you think?'

He lifted his bag and two zips later tossed her a bottle of water. 'Mad that I interfered?'

She held the bottle, absentmindedly running her fingers along the indentations. 'Maybe.' Still she avoided eye contact. 'No.'

Waiting for his turn at the bottle, he stood in front of her. 'Well?'

'Your home.'

That. Not waiting any longer, Athrin lifted the bottle from her hands and took a mouthful. 'I expected it to happen sooner or later. Do not worry.'

Finally, she looked at him, swapping between his eyes and the bottle.

'I offered.'

She snatched the bottle from him.

'It was an old safe house. I know of a few others; we can try to find one,' he said, noticing her hesitance on the bottle still.

Finally, she took a drink then threw it back at him. 'Won't they know of those?'

'I hid them well.' He stowed the bottle in his bag and zipped it back up. 'Probably not.'

'Probably?'

'Not.'

She glared at him. 'You're awfully calm through all this.'

'Panic will get us nowhere.'

'You're mad at me, aren't you?'

Still fiddling with the bag, he looked to her out the corner of his eye. 'Furious.'

'I knew it!' She kicked his shin. 'Why?! Is it because of your hand?' She kicked him again. 'Is it because of the things she said?'

'Lisara…'

'I didn't do anything, Athrin!' She kicked him in the same spot; perfect precision. 'You were the first person the Dragon led me to.' Another kick. 'And I did what people asked or I defended myself!' She reeled back for another, fiercer, kick. But it didn't come. 'I defended myself.' She swung her foot; luckily, it failed to connect. 'I didn't know what to do…'

Athrin put his hand on her head. Her distress concerned him. 'Sorry, Lisara. I was joking.'

This time the kick connected.

'I told you already.' He leaned in a little closer so he could catch her eye. 'I believe you. We will find a way.'

Still glaring at him, and with a slight pout, she nodded. Managing the exchange without another kick.

'Something is missing…' he mumbled, looking at the side of her head.

'My hairpin!' She gasped, tearing from Athrin to pat her hair down in search. 'We have to go back!'

'We cannot.'

'We must. I left it on the dresser!' Urgently, she began tugging his arm down the alley. 'I'll kick that minx in the face!'

'Minx?'

'Athrin!'

He stopped her, leaning over her shoulder and showing her something in the palm of his hand. The hairpin.

'Dumbass!' She snatched it from him and shoved him away. 'Stop trying to joke around, you're terrible at it!' Furiously she fixed it to her hair just above her ear.

Athrin stood in front of her. Perhaps with a sliver of a smile. Perhaps. He had achieved what he wanted. 'In a better mood?'

'Whatever, bro!' She snatched his hand and ran off towards the street. 'Let's go, before you smile or something.'

As they made their way to the street and left the shadows of the alley, they came to a stop. Both of them had seen it. Someone was blocking their path.

Kasari whipped her blade to be within view, making her intent clear. She glared angrily at both of them. 'You cannot hide anymore.' She took some steps forward. 'I will not let you stop me this time, Athrin.'

He could see it. Just as with the tree he had been taught to see it. The mystical nature and anomaly that was the Sorceress; it flowed through her, around her, and her sword. The only known power that could harm the Dragon. And this time she meant it.

'Out of the way, witch,' Lisara snapped. 'We have nothing to do with you, leave us alone.'

'This is my responsibility.' Kasari focused on Lisara now and sneered. 'Why would you involve him when you have caused him so much pain already.'

'Stop that,' Athrin interrupted. Both girls' attention was on him now. 'I chose to stand with Lisara.' His grip tightened around her hand. 'Did you not do the same?'

'After poking around in my head...' Kasari narrowed her eyes at Athrin, angered by his words. 'Don't you dare.'

'Did you not stand with him?'

She began walking towards them, fixated on Athrin. 'I said don't.'

'How is this any different from you and Myan?'

Kasari swung her blade at Athrin. Lisara made to deflect it as she held her sword ready, but the silver blade stopped just at his neck. 'You're trying to bait me, trying to play me using your disgusting ability.'

The blade touched Athrin's neck. He stopped Lisara from responding with a subtle squeeze of her hand.

'What the hell do you know about me? What the hell do you know about Myan?'

It occurred to him. Of course she wouldn't know. How could she? He had only pieced the puzzle together when he touched her sword and saw them. But now, he was sure. She had to know – maybe there was no need to fight. 'I knew Myan well. He was like a brother to me.'

Chapter XVI

When Left Alone

A trickle of blood ran along the razor-sharp silver. Starting at the tip, just as it grazed the skin, and along a third of the blade until it formed a drop, then fell to the ground with an unheard splatter.

In the moment when surprise had set and questions would be surging through her mind, Athrin had grabbed her sword. He ripped it from his neck, grazing himself, and reached for her forehead with his free hand. But Kasari's reflexes were better, now that she knew the danger. Quickly she ducked under his hand, and by releasing her sword, was able to grab his arm and deliver a sharp blow to his elbow and then his ribs. Athrin stumbled back a few feet, leaving Lisara to rush at her in his absence.

Her sword flipped off the ground and found its way back to her hand where she blocked the black blade with ease. She grabbed Lisara's collar and threw her against the wall, snatching the black blade from her grasp in the scuffle. She faced the two of them as they struggled to their feet, both swords in her hands.

This time, she meant it.

'I was told you were once in the Order.' She spoke to Athrin, standing over him menacingly. 'You knew him?'

Athrin tried to stand, but the blow to his ribs shot pain through his entire body with every movement and every breath. Instead, he leaned against the wall and looked up at her. 'I did.' He grunted as he tried to snap his arm back into place. 'He told me what happened with your father. So we left.'

She glared down at him, a volatile cocktail of fury, anger, pity and sadness, boiling up within her eyes.

'I was with him, once, when we met you and your father.' Athrin managed to crack his arm back into place, needing a moment to catch his breath. 'He was always so enamoured with you.' He felt he owed her this explanation after what he had seen and this conversation was buying him the time he needed. 'He could not shut up.' He looked up at her again. There may have been a tear in her eye or a smile on her face; he couldn't tell. 'As you know.'

'I do.' A sliver of a chuckle escaped her. Then she focused again, narrowing her eyes on him. 'How do I know you're not lying to me, that you didn't see all of this in my head?'

'That is not quite how it works…' he muttered, slowly standing using the wall as support. 'But what would you have me tell you?'

Her eyes showed resolve; not once did she look away from him. He knew this was not on a whim – if she was who he thought her to be, he hoped to be able to convince her Lisara was not a threat, that they could find a way. All he needed was to gain her confidence.

'How…' She paused, seemingly reassessing her words and thoughts. 'How did Myan come to the sword?' Her grip tightened around the black blade.

'Ah.' Athrin rested his head on the wall, strength returning to his body but his arm still surging with pain. As to the question posed to him, it was a surprise. No one would know how it happened and she would certainly not have been told by the Order. Athrin knew. He was there. 'It was given to him.' He chose his words carefully; this was not the time nor the place for this conversation. 'He wanted it to fix what he had done.'

By the look on her face Athrin knew she understood what that meant. But still she wasn't satisfied. 'By whom?'

He groaned from the pain, or maybe the question; perhaps both. 'I do want to tell you, Kasari.' With his good arm he propped himself off from the wall and stood on his own two feet. 'Just, this is perhaps not the time.'

'Then you best come with me.' She stepped forward, an amount of the anger subsiding from her voice and brow. 'We can solve this later.'

It was not the worst suggestion he had heard so far; perhaps she was beginning to understand. And that may have been good, he thought. He glanced over to Lisara, prepared to call a parlay on this fight, but something was amiss.

The black blade wrenched from Kasari's grasp, too strong for her to keep grip. It tumbled through the air and slammed to the ground near Lisara who stood not far from them.

'Enough.' A voice came from Lisara's form. It was not dissimilar to her, but darker and colder than it should have been. Lisara plucked the sword from the ground and looked up to them. Her eyes shimmering with a golden glow, replacing the striking blue eyes Athrin had come to know. 'This squabble has gone on for long enough.'

Kasari stood ready, taking her sword in both hands. It appeared she knew what this was. Athrin took a single cautious step forward. 'Lisara, let us go with Kasari and come up with a plan.'

'You have spoken enough, boy.' She turned to Athrin as the words came, and in those eyes he could no longer see Lisara.

'I told you,' Kasari said quickly. 'I knew this would happen.'

The golden gaze found her now, accompanied by a sort of smile. 'Little sorceress.' A step forward. 'How unfortunate to see you again.'

*

The city square was alive with excitement. Filled with people from corner to corner, all cheering and shouting praise as a man walked onto the podium. He wore a perfectly tailored and pressed suit, navy blue and a red tie. He waved to the crowd as he approached the stand prepared for him. Either side of him walked two men in black suits, carefully and quietly protecting him.

Also sharing the podium were a select few attendees. One could have been the mayor, the other a secretary, but one was unlike the others. He stood a head taller than almost everyone else in his immaculate military uniform, his unyielding gaze scanned the surroundings carefully. Artos. Representing the Order. He watched the man in the blue suit, scoffing at the banners that called him president.

Finally, after much waving and pandering, the president reached the stand riddled with microphones and addressed the crowd. 'Good morning Seceena,' he greeted famously. The people cheered and screamed, elated by mere words.

Artos ignored this man's speech, instead scanning the crowd and the buildings surrounding them. Something was coming, he knew as much. All he had to do was wait.

*

Athrin caught Kasari as she fell and helped her up. The two stood not far from Lisara, weary of the next move.

The black blade rested on her shoulder. She tapped it to a rhythm as the golden eyes watched them curiously. 'You aid her when she would readily kill you,' the voice said to Athrin. 'Do you not understand opposition, boy?'

'I did not know he could take control like this,' Athrin said quietly to Kasari. They stood ready.

'I've only seen him do it once.' With a quick motion, Kasari whipped her sword in front of her and took a stance. 'You best leave. He will kill you.'

'What happened to Lisara?' Athrin stepped between them, determined to not allow them a fight.

'It doesn't matter!' Kasari pushed past him to have a clear path at her enemy.

'Of course it matters!' He resisted her advance, keeping her at bay. He wanted answers; he needed answers.

The golden eyes alternated between the two of them, a feeling of disinterest visibly shown. 'The girl is sleeping,' the voice interrupted.

Then there was still a chance, Athrin thought. From Lisara's imposter, he turned to Kasari again. 'If I can bring her back, will you stop trying to kill her?'

'How will that stop him?' she spoke over him angrily, fighting to get through.

'I will find a way.'

A sigh came from Lisara. 'I have entertained this for long enough,' the voice said calmly. 'Goodbye, little sorceress.' The golden eyes glanced over Athrin as a secondary. 'Boy.' Then Lisara began to turn away.

Kasari leapt away from Athrin and at Lisara. The two swords connected and a battle erupted.

It was of the likes Athrin had never seen, the speed and skill with which these two fought surpassed anything a human should be capable of. More than that, the fight seemed so fierce that it could end at any moment, with the loser's life forfeit.

'Why did you come back here?' Kasari snapped, kicking off the wall to propel a strike, but with a thunderous crash, one that was deflected easily. 'Haven't people suffered enough?'

Lisara knocked the silver blade away and ducked under its defences to deliver a quick upward swing, Kasari leapt to the side and out of the way. 'Your suffering is your own,' the voice said.

'It's all your fault!' Kasari dove at Lisara and pinned her to the wall. Their swords linked and all remaining in the path of a deadly blow.

Calmly, the golden eyes searched over Kasari as if looking for something, a neutral expression on Lisara's face. 'My, how you have lost your way.'

Aggression and fury erupted within Kasari at those words. It had struck her more than any sword blow could. In that vulnerable moment, Lisara grabbed her arm and pulled her open to a swift kick that separated them.

'I see you feel it,' the voice continued. 'Doubt.'

Kasari stood angrily, holding her sword ready. 'I have spent years chasing you, preparing for this. There is no doubt.'

'No?' the voice came coldly. Lisara still stood, motionless, expressionless. 'Blinded by hate and rage as you are?'

'For you!' Kasari yelled, tightening her grip and stance, ready to attack. 'Only you.'

'Only?' the voice asked quietly. Slowly, Lisara's shoulders dropped as the tension left her, the golden glow faded from her eyes and a bright blue stare filled with sorrow met Kasari. 'Then why are you trying to kill me?' Lisara cried.

*

The crowd spun into a panic. Many started running, trampling over anyone and anything, a stampede of fear and conceit.

Masked attackers had come, assaulting the Order soldiers seemingly with indifference. Their plan had failed.

Artos and a few men stood around the president on his podium and defended him from the aggressors. 'Do you see now?' he asked the cowering navy blue suit. He looked around the city square and watched as his soldiers routed the attack. 'You came to offer them aid, but like rabid dogs, they'd sooner bite.'

'Thank you, Artos,' the president exclaimed, huddled tightly in fear of the surrounding chaos. 'If you and your men hadn't been here—'

'As I said.' Artos spoke over him; he did not care what the suit had to say. 'We are all that keeps them at bay.'

'Yes, yes.' The president dabbed the sweat from his brow. 'Perhaps, we should discuss the future of the city in full this time.'

Artos stood before the man, nearly twice his size, and looked down on him. 'The future of the city?' He opened his coat and removed a silver pistol from a holster, putting the barrel to the man's forehead in a slow and meticulous motion. The president stared at the barrel and the man holding it, utterly frozen in terror. Artos glared at him with a diluted mixture of disdain and disgust. '*My* city.'

*

The sword nearly slipped from her grasp, but she held it in one hand. She could but stare at Lisara, the black blade, and her own. Rejected or not, those words had affected her. Resounded within her. Leaving her with uncertainty.

'Lisara,' Athrin called, relieved to hear her voice again. More so than he could explain. But then she turned to him, and a familiar icy chill passed through his being.

Tears ran from eyes, consumed in sadness. She forced herself a smile, one he had seen often in their best moments. She fought to speak. 'I'm sorry, honey-bear.' Everything inside of her rejected these words, but she needed to speak them clearly. 'I made him a promise.'

It had returned. That empty hole. Only now did he realise it had been filled. That she had filled it. But now she was leaving, and he would be alone again.

Being alone did not scare him; he was used to it, preferred it even, though maybe he did not fancy it. But the look in her eyes, the tears she shed, that terrified him. More than himself, she would be alone again. 'Lisara,' he called clearly, her blue eyes already fading, but she heard him. 'You still owe me for those shoes.'

She laughed. Wiped her tears. Looked right at him and smiled in that way he had come to depend on.

Then she was gone, replaced by an impostor who merely resembled her. Bright golden eyes scanned the surroundings before settling on Athrin, a look almost resembling resentment within them. 'All of you make me sick,' the dark voice growled.

Athrin made to speak, words of protest, something to deter what came next, anything to stop Lisara from being taken away.

But the voice spoke over him. 'Quiet,' it snapped, with a step to the side, away from Athrin. 'I speak to your hypocrisy.' Lisara turned to

Kasari who made attempts at mustering a stance, or further, resolve. 'And to her dishonour.'

'I will not let you take her,' Athrin said firmly, taking a cautious step forward. He would ignore the words this imposter would use; already he had seen the effectiveness of them.

'She is not some prize to fight for, boy,' the voice said coldly, keenly aware of Athrin's every action and still slowly approaching Kasari. 'Correct your insecurities on your own, instead of placing that burden on another.'

Athrin took another step forward. 'And you call me a hypocrite.'

Those golden eyes narrowed on him like a predator priming for the kill. 'Do not test me, boy.'

'Hit a nerve?' Athrin felt a drop of sweat run from his brow. He readied himself. 'Was Lisara vulnerable enough for the mighty Dragon?'

An uncomfortable moment of silence lingered between them, until the imposter smiled. 'I see what you are doing, boy,' the voice sneered. 'It will take more than that to goad me.'

Athrin took another step forward. As expected, the golden gaze watched him closely, just as he had planned. 'I hope my trust is not misplaced,' he said.

'We'll see.' Kasari swept Lisara from her feet with a leg and raised her sword, ready to pin her to the ground. Athrin lurched forward to assist.

And it very nearly worked. If their enemy was anyone else, it would have. As she fell, Lisara pressed her hand to the ground and flipped herself away from Kasari's blade. In the same movement, she drove the pommel of her sword onto the side of Kasari's head and knocked her away. Once she landed on her feet, she leapt at Athrin and threw him to the wall, pinning him in place by the edge of the blade. The voice growled coldly, 'I have had enough of you.'

Suddenly, screams and shouting erupted around them, the streets beyond the alley filled with people as they ran and scattered. The sound of gunfire could be heard in the distance.

Kasari stood, wiping the blood from the side of her eye. 'What's happening...'

'Ah,' the voice grumbled. 'It begins.'

Athrin grabbed Lisara's arm in one hand and the blade in the other, halting the attempt to behead him, for now.

'What have you done?!' Kasari cried over the rumbling and panic around them.

The voice grumbled angrily, 'You assume my hand at play?'

'Answer me!'

'Your Guildmaster has moved to take the city. He may have killed one of your leaders.'

'Oh no, the president's visit... How could he?'

Lisara's arm jerked forward, but Athrin held fast, suffering only a shallow cut. 'Ask the boy. He has seen the same signs as I.'

Athrin struggled, his grip slipping and the blade digging deeper into his hand and neck.

'Athrin?'

'A little busy...'

'He knew all of it,' the voice sneered, pushing a little more into the blade. 'And did nothing.'

'It had nothing to do with me.'

'Neither does this!' The blade moved deeper, blood seeping from his already wounded hand, the bandage already sliced apart. 'You claim neutrality, but all you are is a coward, huddled in your little bubble of gathered misery.'

The screaming and yelling intensified as more and more people sped through the area. Sirens soon joined the chorus as emergency services began responding. But the Order had made their move already and the gears were now in motion.

'You might be right. Streets may burn, people may struggle.' It became harder for Athrin to breathe now. 'But they have those that will fight for them.' He freed his hand from the grip, the blade dug deep into the side of his neck, but he was able to reach into his pocket and remove the small pouch, a glimmer of red inside, then he touched Lisara's face. 'I am fighting for her.'

Chapter XVII

Anonymous Sacrifice

He had been here before. This was where he wanted to be. Even in this dark and endless void, Athrin recognised it, could feel it – she was close.

Steadily, cautiously, he began to walk. Wading through the darkness he made his way, calling out to her. 'Lisara.' His voice did not echo, swallowed up in the endless nothing. But he kept walking, calling.

'I should have known.' A voice resounded back at him from every direction. The same deep dark voice he had heard before, the air around him grew warmer with each word. 'Reckless fool.'

'I have come for her,' Athrin called into the darkness, turning in circles to spot the beast. 'You cannot stop this.'

The void rumbled and quaked. 'Neither can you.' The rumbling subsided and the voice seemed to recede with it.

Slowly the veil began to give way, to mould and form itself into a shape. The further he walked, the clearer it became. This was his apartment, just as he had left it. Before long, his eyes adjusted and he could see someone by the balcony window, her long blonde hair unmistakeable even in this darkened room.

'Lisara,' Athrin called, hurrying to meet her. But she did not turn to face him, her eyes focused on the view of the city out the window. He stood at her side, part of him relieved to see her safe, and waited.

'Athrin,' she began quietly, gathering the words she wanted to say. This might be her last chance. 'I haven't been entirely honest with you.'

That was no surprise. Athrin could probably count the times she had been truthful on one hand. But her demeanour was different, her shoulders low, her gaze avoiding him, her voice trembling. He waited.

'The Dragon wanted you because…' Lisara clutched the hem of her shirt while she spoke, her grip tightening as she struggled to continue. 'Because of what you can do, so he didn't need me. He didn't want to give me what I wanted.'

A rumble echoed from the distance, perhaps from the city. A subtle tremor could be felt underfoot. Athrin could not see anything amiss from here.

'There are things he wants to do, and all he needs is for someone to take him there.' Lisara lost her words again, this time for longer. The silence around them was almost overwhelming, if not for the irregular rumbling from far away. 'I can do that, at least, and then…'

Athrin waited for her to finish that crucial detail, even realising he had held his breath in anticipation, but she didn't.

'And then?' His prompt was quiet, so quiet he doubted she had even heard him. But she did.

'Then he'll give me what I wanted.'

'And what was that?' He didn't wait for even a moment to pass before asking.

The distant rumbling grew more frequent, louder, and the tremors reverberated through the walls.

And then, finally, Lisara looked at him. Those big blue eyes glittered radiantly, even in the dour light of what could peek through the window. She smiled at him, comforted by just seeing his face, vacant expression or otherwise. Then she answered him, no lies or half-truths, for the first time. 'I wanted to die.'

The building shook, the supports creaked and the rumbling brought forth a thundering crash. Athrin could see it through the window, amongst the buildings of the city, something had burst up from the ground. The earth gave way and parted as a tremendous beast writhed beneath the surface. A great dragon burst through and reared its head, clawing the rest of the way until it emerged fully.

The creature's scales a deep black, shining with a deep blue hue in the light of the rising sun. Brilliant golden eyes snapped open as the beast surveyed its surroundings, an immense tail flailed around it while it gathered itself.

From its back, massive wings unfurled and brushed aside small trees, cars, and all debris in the gale that followed. The creature reared its head and let out a roar, a roar which echoed throughout the entire city and even beyond.

Athrin looked on as the city he knew crumbled just outside of his window. He watched as the breast took a deep breath and expelled flames that swept through streets and highways. And in that instant, Seceena was on fire.

Lisara placed her hand on the glass as she watched the colossal creature weave flames through the city. It terrified her. She would not wish such a fate upon anyone, and so, it has to be her.

The building shook again, the walls barely holding back the chaos and devastation happening just beyond the glass pane. Athrin's gaze fell upon Lisara again, her small frame huddled and quiet. This was unlike her. This was the girl that nearly burnt down his kitchen, the girl that bought boots with a pilfered wallet, the very same girl that woke him up from his melancholy on a cold, rainy evening with a pointy object... very pointy.

'Lisara.'

His sudden snap startled her. She took her fingers from the glass, but did not dare look at him. All she could see was a reflection of his silhouette in the glass.

There were so many things he should have said, so much he would elucidate if he could. But, right now, there was only one thing he wanted to know. 'What do you want right now?'

Another tremendous roar echoed through the city and even shook the foundation of the building. The very air felt warmer than before as the desolation outside crept closer but it did not interrupt them.

Lisara sniffed loudly, fighting to hold something back as it ran from her eyes. But she could not deny it anymore. 'I want to go home.'

After a moment, Athrin made to speak, to interject, add, or inquire, but he never had the chance.

Suddenly, Lisara turned and leapt at him, wrapping her arms around his neck, and possibly cutting off his air supply. 'I want to learn how to cook.' He knew it. 'I want different boots.' Uh oh. 'I want to talk shit late into the night.' Okay, sure. 'I want to go home.' She hiccupped, quickly stomping on his foot as if it was his fault, all his fault. 'With you.'

Truth be told, he was not expecting that reaction. Once the surprise had passed, Athrin moved to put a hand on her shoulder, add a comforting touch while he formulated some kind of response. But before he could, Lisara released him and took a step back.

'But I can't,' she muttered quietly, holding him at arm's length with all of her strength.

'Why?'

'Because…' Then, she pushed him and he tumbled back into the dark abyss he had started from. 'I made a promise.'

*

Athrin was falling. He wasn't sure how long he had been here, in this empty void, and it didn't matter. Nothing mattered anymore. In fact, it had been that way for such a long time.

There were times when he thought he was on the right path, better times, but those moments were fleeting, and he would always end up right back where he started. But, maybe it didn't matter. Maybe, this was how it was meant to be.

Though, there was something else. Something he had forgotten, like an itch he just couldn't quite reach. He had promised someone something. His quest.

The void began to take shape once again, forming shapes around him and morphing into a room, a familiar room, one straight from his nightmares.

The room, dark and stifling, had the scent of fresh blood lingering in the air. In the centre was what appeared to be a crude operating table with tools, beakers and various apparatuses encircling it. Everything soaked in blood. The floor was riddled with corpses, or parts of, with a trail leading from the single entrance and staircase to this apparent crypt. A few of the bodies were outfitted in white lab coats, stained in red.

In a corner of this room was movement, the only two people alive in the entire building. One was a marginally younger Athrin. His hair was shorter and neater, less stubble dotted around his jawline. He was slumped on the ground and in his arms he held the body of a woman. A trail of blood followed her from the table. Brilliant auburn-golden hair flowed around her. The blood and grime of this place did nothing to detract from its gleam. Athrin clutched her tightly, frantically; the look in his eyes was that of desperation and tremendous fear.

'I'm sorry.' He pressed his head to hers. 'I'm sorry,' he whispered over and over. 'If only I'd gotten here sooner.'

'Athrin.' Her voice was frail, her eyes unfocused and blankly gazing up at the light bulb swaying from the ceiling. As she reached for him, he grabbed her hand tightly. 'You did nothing wrong.'

'I wasn't there.' He examined her wounds, looking for something, anything to avoid what he already knew. He knew it was too late. 'I was—'

'Helping people,' she interrupted him, stopping him completely. She always had that power. 'Questing for civility?' She smiled and her eyes found his at last, a fading light deep within them. 'Good boy.'

'I will find who did this,' he assured her in a quieter voice, one entirely without emotion. 'And I will kill all of them.'

'No, Athrin.' Her smile vanished and her brow pinched into a frown, for but a moment, before her gaze softened again. 'You are better than that.' With her free hand she reached for something, grasping it tightly once her weakened fingers had found it. 'This is what they wanted.' She handed him a blood-red gemstone, almost as large as her fist. Yet it fit in the palm of his hand. 'Take it. One day you will need it.'

'Don't. Please.' His voice was quieter, struggled. 'I won't know what to do without you.'

She touched the side of his face and smiled again, her movements slower. He grabbed her hands. 'You'll find the way.'

'Amber. Please.'

'Athrin…' She struggled to speak as her voice failed. 'Please. Don't let this…' Her grip on his hands began to slip away, and quiet tears ran from her eyes. 'Don't give up on people.'

Then all was silent. Insurmountably so.

'Amber,' he whispered. But knew she would not answer.

The expressionless, unfeeling demeanour he always wore slowly fell away, and he began to struggle, as if feeling for the first time. He gripped her tightly and held her close in an embrace that could not be returned.

He cried out, emptied his lungs, such as he had never before. He could no longer bottle these things he had ignored; the things he had not been able to see.

For the first time, he understood.

Athrin watched the contorted image of himself on the floor, desperately clutching to someone lost. Something he would continue to do. He had not ever let go. Even now, he realised, he couldn't.

*

Silence, for what felt like an eternity. But he could feel something boiling within him, sense that something was different. And he knew he was alive; there was still much he had to do. Death was not allowed.

'Athrin,' the voice whispered.

He tried to move, but there was no response from his body.

'Athrin.' The voice grew a little more desperate, as if concerned.

He sought to answer this call still, for he could never and would never be able to deny her call. But it was no longer because it was all he had left, he wanted to answer, there were things he had to finish.

'Get up!'

*

His eyes snapped open. This ceiling was not familiar to him. He shot up, and immediately a pain coursed through his body but he ignored it, there were other concerns. 'Lisara,' he called, looking around the room for signs of her as his eyes adjusted.

'She's not here.'

Beside him sat Kasari. This was an infirmary; her presence allowed him to make some deductions and figure out where he likely was.

'Finished?' She tried to draw his attention again, but his focus was elsewhere. 'Do you know where you are?'

'An Order hall.' He checked the door; it was on the other side of the room. An emergency exit would be difficult, but possible. 'Where is Lisara?'

'The Dragon is gone,' Kasari began, subtly shifting in her seat to intercept him if he attempted to flee. 'And you only barely escaped death.'

Athrin checked his injuries, and though they had been dressed and tended to, he was not in good condition. A familiar smell of the salves and antidotes, the same as the ones he still kept, were evidence that Kasari wanted him alive, at least. But the wound on his neck threatened to split open at any moment. 'What happened to Lisara?'

'The Dragon disappeared,' she said sternly, as if correcting him. 'Artos has forced the city into lockdown and we're scrambling for information.' Kasari locked onto him with an ice-cold stare and held it. 'Information I think you have.'

'My concern is with Lisara.'

'Athrin.' With a stern voice, Kasari captured his attention, enough that she might correct him. 'She is gone. It's the Dragon now. Take my advice, if you do nothing else, and remember that fact.'

It was clear to him that her intentions for him were not hostile, a stark contrast to their previous encounter, but he would not accept it.

Athrin took a deep breath, his entire body ached as he did, but he calmed himself. 'I will not accept that.'

'I didn't either,' she began, a solemn tinge in her tone, and an indescribable glint within her eyes. 'And I regretted it.'

He knew what lurked within her, if only by her eyes – it was as if he was looking into a mirror.

'Myan.'

Just hearing that name affected her, and she showed it for but a moment before locking it away. Athrin knew pieces of what had happened, but even though he and Myan were close friends, they had not spoken in many years after going their separate ways. If he was going to get some kind cooperation from her, he would need to reach even a semblance of understanding with her.

'What happened to him?'

Such a simple question, but merely the thought of recounting those events caused Kasari to withdraw almost completely, and revert to the cold façade which she showed to most people. 'We're not here for story time, Athrin. We have a problem and I need information from you.'

'Then we will trade stories.'

'You are in no position to barter with me.'

'And you think the reverse is true?'

Kasari may have smirked; it was impossible to tell. He was well accustomed to interrogations, from both sides of the table, but it seemed so was she. All the stories about the ice-queen sorceress were true.

'Hanson was right, you like to push buttons.' Kasari leaned forward slightly while maintaining strict eye-contact. 'What's your affiliation with Calem?'

Even if the stories were true, to some extent, Athrin knew better. He knew there was another side to her, all through stories from his old friend, whether he wanted to hear them or not. 'We agreed to see other people.'

'Athrin.'

'What happened on that rooftop, Kasari?'

This time, the smirk was visible. She tossed something in front of him and he recognised it immediately: the small pouch he had in his pocket.

Now partially unwrapped, a glimmering blood-red stone could be seen inside.

'Want to tell me about that?' Kasari sneered, knowing full well she had placed him in check.

Athrin closed it, concealing the stone, but left it in the open. 'Not particularly.'

'That's fine.' Still, Kasari did not break eye contact, but her tone was now a little gentler. 'I already know where you got it.'

Athrin's grip closed around the stone. It was his turn to put her in check, even if it felt underhanded. 'I can see why he was a little scared of you.'

'Only a little?'

Kasari surprised him when she smiled. He was not expecting that. 'Kasari…' he began, thinking through his words and lining them up as best he could. 'What happened to Myan was—'

She spoke over him, interrupting him entirely and easily. 'Those people that harvested these stones used them to drive the Dragon into frenzy and consume what was left of Myan.'

Athrin could do nothing but stare at her as she spoke, that icy façade had returned, even colder than before.

'I let it rampage and kill people because I thought there was a chance he…' She stood abruptly, catching and correcting her lapse. 'I killed it.'

Athrin saw that flash in her eyes, for but an instant. Something familiar.

'If you won't tell me what I need to know, I will make my own way. Last time, I hesitated. I will not make that mistake again.'

CHAPTER XVIII

THE ABSOLUTE

Athrin was left alone in the room. Kasari had already gone after having said her piece. He suspected the aim was to keep him here, to avoid his further interference in her quest. No doubt, this was the reason for the guards standing just outside, who he could occasionally hear chatting and shuffling restlessly.

Normally, escaping such a situation would be readily achievable, not trivial, but possible. Unfortunately, he was in no condition to take any reckless actions; his wounds were severe and his opposition were anything but amateurs. He would need to plan his escape.

Though, just as he had stood and began to gather his things, the door opened and a familiar face entered the room. It was entirely out of reflex, from the days long past, but the remembered respect had not waned; Athrin immediately stood at attention and saluted the man, his injuries may have stung due to the abrupt movement, but he didn't think twice.

Closing the door behind him, the man had not yet noticed Athrin. He was tall and wide-shouldered, intimidating to almost anyone who stood in the shadow of his presence. That is, until he would speak.

'Lieutenant Guyvan,' Athrin greeted properly, maintaining his salute perfectly.

'Oh no, no, I am not a lieutenant anymore…' He stopped halfway across the room, finally looking at and noticing Athrin. His brow scrunched under concentrated thought as he perused his memory, aiding the process by scratching his grey-speckled beard. And then, he placed the memory, and his face lit up with excitement. 'Athrin?' He stomped the rest of the way to Athrin and grabbed his shoulders to shake a better view out of him. 'I had no idea it was you, laddie!' His bellowing laughter filled the room from wall to wall. 'How long has it been?'

'Quite a while…' Athrin struggled to speak without a pained lilt to his voice. He had forgotten about Guyvan's renowned bear-like-grip. 'Sir.'

Realising finally that Athrin was injured, though arguably a few moments too late, Guyvan released him but his delight did not wane. 'I haven't seen you since… well… since…' His words trailed off somewhat, as more and more memories came flooding back at the sight of a familiar face. Then he smiled gently and lightly tapped Athrin's shoulder. 'My condolences, lad.'

'Thank you, sir.' Athrin straightened his arm. A dull pop from the socket told him all was right again. 'And to you too.'

'My thanks, lad,' Guyvan responded with a nod and a solemn tone. 'Myan's passing has been… difficult. More so for some than others.'

An uncomfortable silence lingered for a moment, allowing them both to gather their thoughts, wits and winds.

'Well, when the lass told me to keep an eye on the chap in this room, I was not expecting her caution to be so well justified.' Guyvan chuckled heartily, his friendly tone at odds with the subjects at hand, but that was to be expected from him. 'Tell me, lad…' His voice sharpened suddenly, but was not quite hostile. 'What's going on?'

Athrin knew well that Guyvan was gauging what he knew, as well as attempting to establish motive. His reputation preceded him, even if he was no longer within the ranks of the Order. He was known to be one of the best leaders they had, and his talents for information gathering and espionage were peerless. But Athin did not have the time for subtlety. 'The Dragon has someone, and I have to find her before Kasari does.'

'These last few years the lass has made it her mission to hunt the Dragon. As the sorceress, it is her duty to do so.'

'Why?'

'It's what the sorceress has always done, lad, like those before her. She is the only one who can.'

'That does not mean Lisara has to die.'

'Lisara?' Guyvan searched his memory banks, his brow contorting as it always did. That name was familiar. 'Bartram's lass?' As the pieces fell into place, more and more began to make sense. But it didn't matter for the subject at hand. 'She has made her choice, lad.'

'No,' Athrin interrupted sternly. Having just recently realised it himself, he had to make something very clear. 'Lisara did not ask for this. This is happening to her because I turned the offer down.'

Guyvan watched Athrin as he spoke and shuffled restlessly. Though he didn't show it, he was surprised to see Athrin this way.

'I know there is another way.' Athrin spoke slowly, choosing his words carefully under the unyielding gaze of Guyvan. 'And Kasari should not have to face this alone.'

For as long as he had known him, Athrin was always soft-spoken and professional. He never spoke out of turn and always did as he was told, sometimes to a fault. Guyvan looked at his left hand, losing himself in a wave of melancholy for but a moment before clenching a tight fist. 'Young folk shouldn't have to carry all this weight.' Finally, he let out a long sigh and faced Athrin once again. 'Artos has forced the city into lockdown. Moving around may be difficult. The lass said she would begin with the Girdan, to gather information.'

'Thank you, sir.'

'Athrin,' Guyvan began suddenly, wearing a more serious expression and matching tone. Athrin had never seen that look in this man's

eyes before. 'Kasari is a good kid. I have failed her twice in her life…
tremendously. Please don't make this be the third.'

*

The old dilapidated hotel surged in chaos, much like the state of the
city outside the walls, as people hurried from room to room in search of
their comrades or belongings as they scrambled, to not only make sense
of what was happening, but prepare for the worst and fight or flee at a
moment's notice if required.

Kasari went mostly unnoticed as she slowly walked down the hallway.
She watched as several injured were brought in and carried to a makeshift
med bay. A spotted trail of red led to the doorway where many overworked
and panicked hands tried to do what they could for the wounded.

A few more doors down and Kasari found who she was looking for.
He sat alone in the corner, hunched shoulders and matted hair matched
the fog of despair hanging over him. He stared blankly at the wall and
did not notice Kasari enter the room or even once she was standing
beside him.

'Calem,' she called gently. She could hardly imagine what would be
going through his mind right now. But she could do nothing to help
him.

After a while his empty stare found her. On any other day he would
have been beside himself in excitement at her presence and his words
gushing with nothing but admiration and praise. But he had nothing
left to offer her. 'Ah, Sorceress.' He sat up, not having quite enough
willpower to stand just yet. 'What brings you to these hallowed halls?'

Kasari shut out the disorder around them, ignored the cries for help
and suffering. As best she could. She had a singular purpose now. 'I've
come to talk to "her".'

In response, Calem let out a grunt, the closest thing to a scoff or
chuckle he could muster. 'In case you haven't noticed; this is not the best
time.'

'You said once I returned to the city I could see her.'

'That was before I knew the city would be on fire.'

'I just want to ask her some things, Calem. I won't harm her.'

'One of her outbursts is the last thing I need right now. Come back another day.' He twisted a sneer into a smile as he spoke, his usual consideration for company well-worn after the last few days.

'Calem, I just need to talk to her.'

'Go away.'

'Calem… please.'

'Go… away…' He pushed out his words through clenched teeth. 'I don't need this right now.'

'This is your fault, Calem,' Kasari said simply, straightening her footing and preparing for the confrontation she was hoping to avoid. 'I warned you against it.'

'You think I don't know that?!' Now Calem stood, shot out of the chair and turned towards Kasari. Though he wouldn't dare lay a finger on her, he knew better. 'You don't think I knew the risks, what would happen if it went wrong?' he shouted angrily, without a care as to who was listening or how far his voice carried. This had been bottled for long enough. 'They forced my hand! How was I to know the psychopath would kill the damn president and blame us?! We were supposed to catch him and demand our rights!' Calem kicked the chair away in his rage.

'Calem!' Kasari tried to quell his anger but it was clear he wasn't even listening to anyone anymore.

'And you!' He pointed a finger at Kasari, channelling all the fury he could not inflict upon her through the futile gesture. 'You and your squabble on that rooftop over broken pebbles, you and that witch left me with this mess. So don't you dare pretend this isn't also your fault!'

'I have nothing to do with this.'

'Nothing?' With gritted teeth, Calem growled angrily. 'Nothing, huh?' He nodded to himself, feeling like he was suffocating in the absurdity of it all. 'You want to see her? Then let's. Let's see what she has to say about all of this.'

Calem charged from the room, leading Kasari further down the hall. He shunned any who came near to him with either a briefing or message, dismissing everything else but his current rage. A few doors down he came to the makeshift holding cells, quickly shouting at the lone guard and chasing him away, before entering with Kasari.

All the cells here were empty, save for one. Huddled in the corner was a woman. She was curled up into as small a shape as she could muster and had not yet noticed their approach, or at least, had not yet reacted to it.

'Elanee,' Calem snapped, shaking the barrier between them to get her attention. 'You have a guest.'

The woman's huddled shape turned further away from them, inaudible mutters her only response or acknowledgement of their presence.

'Elanee,' Calem called again, but when he still didn't receive a reply, his frustration peaked and he stepped aside, gesturing for Kasari to approach instead, if that was her want. 'Do what you will.'

Kasari approached cautiously and recognised her instantly. Even though she had last seen her quite some time ago, she could never forget this woman. But she seemed different. Not the assertive leader or confidant antagonist from before, but withered and withdrawn. 'Elanee,' she began gently, as best she could, still while listening intently to make out the mutterings coming from her. 'It's me, Kasari.'

All it took was for that name to reach her ears and the muttering stopped. Elanee lifted her head ever so slightly and peeked out at Kasari with one eye. A lifetime's worth of hate and anger glared at Kasari, a glimmer of what this woman once was, but most of it was drowned in a thick haze of delusion and sorrow. It faded after a moment and she turned away again, returning to her quiet muttering.

It was hard to believe. Kasari thought her reunion with this woman would have been very, very different. She turned to Calem, who seemed to have calmed down and appeared a little more solemn than before. 'What's wrong with her?'

Calem shrugged. 'She's been like this ever since that day on the rooftop. Something in her snapped, I guess seeing all of your comrades being torn to shreds before your eyes will do that to most people.' He gave Kasari a quick sneer, having some of his anger left over. 'Most people, at least.'

Kasari ignored his remark and refocused her attention on the huddled form in the corner. 'Elanee, since that day I have waited a long time to speak with you. I have been to many places, seen the aftermath the Dragon has left behind. Expectedly, frustratingly, I am no closer to understanding what he wants.' She didn't care if her words could be heard or not – a small part of her had been waiting to say this. To anyone. 'You know something about him. You called out to him. Why?'

The mutterings grew louder and wilder but remained incoherent.

'For some reason he keeps returning to this city and you might know why.' Kasari inched closer to her, keeping her voice calm. 'It wasn't just for Myan, you know something. Please Elanee, tell me why.'

The mutterings continued, steadily increasing. Calem looked on from the sidelines in silence, speechless and curious what she might say.

'Elanee, why is he in Seceena? Why here?' Kasari asked a little louder, eager to get her answer and if not, to move on. 'What does the Dragon want in this city?'

Suddenly, Elanee shot to her feet and looked directly at Kasari, her emotions overflowing. 'You!' Her voice was hoarse but sharp. 'It wants you, witch! You along with that gravestone!'

Kasari did not move, now face to face with this woman and only the bars between them.

'Always the Sorceress, it's always you! Even Myan chose you over me! Me!' Tears streamed down Elanee's face as she screamed at Kasari. All of the frustration, all of the sorrow she had bottled up came flooding out of her in this moment. 'Me…' But then, as the words settled on her tongue, the sadness was quickly overwhelmed by the lingering rage. 'But you killed him!'

'That was no longer Myan,' Kasari interrupted her quickly.

'You killed him!'

'I stopped the thing you caused.'

'You killed him!'

'No…'

'You *killed* him!'

'Fine!' Kasari's hands shook. 'I killed him!' The room fell silent. 'I had to! No one else could, no one else was doing anything to stop him, no one else was...' She was suddenly out of breath. 'So I killed him.'

No one moved, no one spoke, surprised as they were by Kasari's reaction. None of them had ever seen her shed a tear.

Kasari looked Elanee in the eye. And, even if only for this moment, they shared something. 'You don't think I'd take it back if I could?'

A longer moment of silence passed, long enough for Calem to muster his courage and step forward, about to say something, when she did instead.

After a deep breath, Kasari spoke again. 'I have my answer.' With a single quick movement, she wiped her eyes on her sleeve and turned to leave the room. 'All both of you have ever done is blame someone else for your mistakes, shifting it from person to person over the years. You can blame me if you want. I don't care. I'm done.'

*

Athrin took his hand from the tree. He now knew where to go and what to do, more or less.

As he left the park, a shower had started, dark ominous clouds gathered over the city as if to mimic the state of the populous beneath.

He walked carefully from street to street, avoiding the patrolling troops and police as best he could. No one who could avoid it strayed outside. The lockdown was ruthless, indiscriminate and absolute.

It would not take long and the shower would turn into a full downpour. Athrin knew he would need to hurry. As his pace quickened, he began the usual process of planning out his coming mission, a method he would often practice in the past, deliberating on all the possible outcomes and strategies.

But this was not like those times. There was no clear start, no documented outcome or completion criteria. He was out of his depth and he knew it. Yet, he pushed forward. His feet did not stop and his determination did not waver. With barely a plan in mind and hardly a clue as to how, he didn't once stop to reconsider. It was very unlike him, he realised, thinking then that perhaps he had spent too much time around such people and their bad influence. So be it. He decided that after all of this, when he once again stood beside the one responsible, he'd let her know.

By now the downpour had become so fierce he was forced down the alleyways and back streets. Perhaps not a bad turn of events, this weather would make it more difficult for anyone to see him or give chase. Something he was not entirely confident he could avoid more than once in his current condition.

Athrin turned a corner and jogged halfway down the alleyway before coming to a stop. He had reached his first stop already. And surprisingly, she was not on the move; instead, she sat against the wall under the shelter of a dilapidated sheet cover.

He approached carefully, stopping a few feet from her, enough of a distance that he could still react should she lash out at him. And he was not entirely confident she wouldn't. 'Kasari... are you okay?'

Kasari's vacant expression turned to him and only after a few seconds did her vision sharpen and she realise that she was no longer alone. She let out a long sigh. 'Oh, Guyvan... I should have asked Zieg.' She turned away from Athrin, resting her head on her knees. 'Go away, Athrin. I'm just catching my breath.'

'You look like hell.' With few other options for staying dry, Athrin stood beside her, forgoing the safe distance between them and hoping he wouldn't regret it.

'Gee, thanks,' she mumbled in response, not quite able to muster enough energy to portray her annoyance. After hearing some rustling, she realised he had joined her and was making himself comfortable. 'Athrin... what are you doing?'

'Just catching my breath.'

She couldn't believe it. Every encounter they had so far, she was sure to be deliberately callous and cold. Yet he kept appearing again and again. 'You get that we're basically enemies, right?'

'I do not see it that way.'

'Then how do you see it?'

'Well…'

'You know what, never mind. I don't care.' Kasari returned to her state of disregarded hostility.

The rain poured from the gutters and clambered to the paving all around them, drowning out any other sound, any other event. It may have been tranquil, if not for the known threat looming through the veil.

Athrin peeked over to Kasari. Her wet hair clung to her face and neck, but the smart ponytail definitely must have helped. Needless to say, she seemed conflicted; something which Athrin was strangely hoping for. It meant there was hope she might listen.

'Shouldn't you be chasing your girlfriend before I do?' Kasari asked suddenly.

'She is not my girlfriend.' Athrin's response was almost instinctive, fed by a momentary bubble of forgotten frustration.

Kasari tilted her head to the side, enough to meet Athrin's gaze, glaring at him and rivalling the fury of the storm around them. If looks could kill.

Athrin's gulp would have been audible. He wasn't sure what had caused this, but his body demanded he flee, though he couldn't.

'Rather frivolous of you,' Kasari sneered. 'Wasn't she wearing your shirt?'

'Nothing happened,' Athrin cut in quickly, hoping to earn back the little bit of goodwill he might have gained, but he knew this misunderstanding was potently convincing and he would have little chance. 'She did that on purpose, because she knows it annoys me.'

Kasari glare began to sear a mark into his soul, but just before any lasting damage was done, she let out a rather decisive 'humph' and returned to watching the rain again.

Now allowed to breathe a sigh of relief, Athrin did so, letting out a deep breath. But, before he could take another, he heard her voice again, though this time her words were quieter, gentler, as if she didn't particularly want anyone to hear them.

'You remind me of him.'

Athrin dared not speak. He could see the glint in her eyes, that familiar flicker that he would see the few times he caught himself in a mirror. Like a weakened flame struggling in a light breeze.

'Though he talked more.' A frail smile emerged at the thought of something distant. 'A *lot* more.'

The downpour continued overhead. It could have even grown more intense; neither of them paid it any more attention – it may as well have been a gentle shower.

'He could never mind his own business.' A drop of rain fell to her head but she didn't notice. It ran down the side of her hair and along her cheek. 'He was…'

Kasari whispered so quietly, so hesitantly, as if it had slipped out on its own despite herself. But Athrin didn't need to hear it to know. He knew it well.

'I miss him so much.'

CHAPTER XIX

THE WIDENING SHADOW

The sound of the rain flooded in. It was deafening, constant and unrelenting.

Athrin watched a gutter, not too far away, struggle and sway as it guided the torrent to an already overflowing drain. Out the corner of his eye he could almost make out the silhouette of the spectre that followed him, gleefully frolicking and giggling in the rain. He turned again to Kasari, her gaze still drifting out towards the rain. Perhaps she saw a spectre of her own out there.

There were so many things vying for his attention right now, so many places he had to be instead of here, so many avenues he should have pursued instead of this one, but he knew he had to be here. This was important. Not for him, not for the city, not for Lisara, but for his old friend, and for Kasari.

'I do too.'

Kasari remained still and though she did not face him, she was listening.

'He was there, that night.' Athrin spoke slowly, his hesitance not from caution, but remorse. 'He helped me find Amber, when she was taken.' He had never told anyone this before. No one had asked. 'I blamed myself, for all of it.' Part of him still did. 'But he picked me up and told me to do what she said, because she would have chosen those words for a reason.'

'What did she say?'

Kasari was looking at him now and Athrin held her gaze this time. 'Not to give up on people.' It was surprisingly difficult for him to tell someone all this. Though, if anyone deserved to know, it would have been her.

He had begun to realise this recently, more so in this moment, that this is what Amber had been trying to tell him. Not some vague notion of civility or mannerisms, but rather tolerance and acceptance. Something she had always said he had the capacity for. And who was he to argue.

'Kasari,' Athrin began again, just before he had lost her gaze. 'He loved you. Do not forget it.'

Kasari remained fixed on Athrin, searching his eyes for motive or pretence. But there was none; perhaps she had seen the same as he, the shimmer of something familiar. Those ice-cold eyes softened ever so slightly, just enough that Athrin knew something had changed.

'Okay.'

He was not expecting that. Though, honestly, he had no idea what to expect.

'Don't lose your way, huh…' Kasari mumbled to herself, sweeping soaked hair behind her ear. She cleared her throat, suppressing what threatened to rise to the surface. 'So, I assume you have a plan?'

Not at all. But this was far more than he could have hoped for; with Kasari's help, there might be a chance.

'Athrin…'

Of course, there was a catch.

'You have one chance to do whatever it is you want to do.' Kasari refocused his attention, quickly curbing his expectations. 'Then we have to stop her.'

*

The Seceena City Military Force, ominously known as the Order within the right circles, had all but seized control of the city. The downpour did little but slow their progress, after all, they had prepared for this day.

Artos stood alone by the large window of his office and looked down across the city from his high-rise vantage point. Streaks of rain pulled across the glass, like a shroud over his accomplishment. Had he the capacity, he may have smiled proudly.

The hushed ambience of the tapping rain was interrupted by footsteps from the other side of the office, slowly and deliberately announcing a presence.

Surprised, or perhaps impressed, Artos watched the silhouette of a person in the reflection of the glass. Still clothed in the darkness, he could at least tell it was not one of his people. They stopped far enough away for him to react if required.

'My guards have disappointed me,' Artos growled calmly. In the reflection, he noticed the sheen of a weapon in this interloper's hand. 'An assassin?' He let out a disinterested sigh, having already expected such an attempt after today's events; it was unavoidable.

However, the intruder did not respond, nor did they approach further.

'One of Calem's, I take it?' Artos scoffed at the very thought, almost choking at the mere mention of such an inconsequential dreg. 'The Girdan, is that what you call yourselves?'

Still, there was no answer.

Offended by the silence to his demands, Artos turned to face this trespasser, that he might get a better look at them. Only, once he had turned around, this person was now standing just across his desk.

In an instant, Artos reflexively drew his pistol and held it ready. He could feel something wasn't right. But, he did not pull the trigger. Now that he could see the intruder more clearly, he recognised her.

It was a young woman. With long blonde hair, sopping wet and clinging to her face, neck and shoulders. She was looking directly at him but there was something peculiar about her eyes.

'Bartram's girl.' Artos lowered his weapon just enough that he would still be able to defend himself yet see her more clearly. 'Lisara, was it? I knew your father. A shame what happened to your family.'

Of all the people he would have anticipated to appear before him, now of all times, she was not who he could have expected. Her presence was entirely a mystery. Then, now that she was closer, he got a better glimpse of the weapon she held. A black blade, almost invisible in the dark. It felt familiar.

'What is it you seek?'

She spoke suddenly, her tone sharp and cold, at odds with the pretty face. Artos knew this girl. He had seen her several times alongside her father at the banquets and gatherings of the upper echelons in the city and yet now, she seemed to be someone else entirely.

'You have schemed, you have plotted and now you have my attention.'

Artos' eyes widened as the realisation came to him. He couldn't believe it, after all these years. It had finally happened.

The girl's eyes were locked onto his, a golden glow within them, a striking shimmer against the dark shadows wrapped around her.

'What is it you seek?'

The golden glow, the consuming shadow, the ominous presence, now Artos was certain, this is what he had been waiting for, this is what he had been fighting for. 'I want what is mine.' Everything he had done led to this moment. 'I want what is owed to me. I want what I have fought for.' The Dragon had come to him at last. 'I want what is my destiny.'

'To this end you have schemed with your allies.' As the words reached his ears, a flash of the past appeared before Artos' eyes. First of the people he once called comrades, the generals of his Order. 'You have conspired with your enemies.' Next came the vision of a woman who stood shoulder to shoulder alongside her masked compatriots. 'Toyed with ancient magic you could not understand.' Then the scene of a rooftop appeared before him, the gravelled path strewn with glowing red stones. 'You have even stolen the name of an old king.' Finally, a vision of a different time opened before him, an ancient city mighty and powerful, the castle towered over the surrounding structures. But everything was on fire. 'Arrogance.' A final flash and Artos' consciousness had returned to his office, slightly off balance from the surreal images.

He regained his footing, looking around quickly to find nothing had changed. The girl was still across the table from him, glaring at him as before. 'Arrogance?' Artos shook the last of the mist from his mind, a tinge of anger bubbling up inside of him. 'It is ambition. That which draws you!'

'Oh?'

'You are here, answering my call.' Artos had abandoned pretences. He was so close he could feel it. 'All I have done, all I have sacrificed, was for this moment.'

'Then you are also a fool.'

Artos fell silent, taken aback by the response to his efforts. 'Have I not earned it?' There had to be some misunderstanding. 'Decades spent crawling around in the shadows looking for the trail of your legend.' He could not be denied. It had to be a mistake. 'Blood and money spent in equal measure to seize control of the city. Dregs I was forced to align with to achieve a chance, only to be thwarted by Guyvan's damn boy and that sorceress.' All he had done meant something; it had purpose, it had meaning and it was to be justified. 'And yet, finally, here you are before me... if not to make a deal, then why?'

The Dragon remained fixated on Artos, eyeing him as if contemplating his very existence in the world, and bewildered by it.

'Curiosity.'

The rain pounded on the window. Streaks of ambient light fluttered across the floor, cast through the veil of water against the glass. Amidst the ambient quiet, a sharp metallic click echoed from wall to wall.

Artos raised his loaded weapon and pointed it at the transgressor to his destiny. Fury overwhelmed his senses, spurred on by his indomitable will and inexhaustible pride. He would not be denied.

A thunderous crack erupted through the fallen silence, for but a moment, before receding again behind the veil.

*

Athrin followed Kasari through the familiar corridors of The Order building. Both of them had once frequented this place. Both of them disliked the thought of returning to it. But the trail had led them here.

'It's too quiet,' Kasari whispered as they turned another corner and continued on.

'Considering what is happening outside, it is not entirely a surprise.'

'But on Artos' floor?'

'He would often chase people away.'

'True...'

'But I agree with you.' They approached the door to Artos' office, as imposing as ever. 'Way too quiet.'

Unprompted, both took up position on either side of the door. Kasari quietly unsheathed her sword and after a firm nod to Athrin, they breached the office.

With a quick and precise attack, Kasari slashed across the door, bypassing the lock and allowing Athrin to kick open the door. They burst inside, readying themselves for immediate confrontation but were not prepared for what was waiting for them.

A large section of the window had been cracked and shattered, rain trickled in and pooled on the floor, mixing with a trail of blood.

Artos' pistol lay on his desk, still held firmly in his grip, though severed from his body. Not far from it, he had collapsed to his knees. The man had long since passed, held up only by the sword protruding from his neck. The black blade.

'Just as your namesake; a fool,' the Dragon said calmly, even knowing the words would not be heard. 'Mistaking the sacrifices of others as your own. Confusing ambition with greed.'

With a quick movement, the Dragon whipped the blade free. The body remained where it was, and did not move. Nor would it again.

'Lisara!' Athrin called desperately. He was relieved to see her again even if it was clear she was still not in control.

The Dragon watched interestedly as the blood crawled across the floor, and just before touching Lisara's bare feet, hoisted up and sat on the office desk. The Dragon looked straight at them, those golden eyes glowing ominously through the heavy shadows.

'What have you done?!' Kasari called out, her focus still on the slain Order leader and the consequences this would bring.

'Tying up loose ends,' The Dragon growled, thick with indifference.

'What?'

'You do not need to understand.'

'When this gets out—'

A loud clang echoed through the office, interrupting Kasari and shifting her attention. The Dragon had driven the tip of the blade into the floor and leaned against the pommel. 'I killed this man, little sorceress. No one else shall claim it.'

'It's not that simple…'

'Artos knew…' Athrin spoke up, watching the Dragon perched upon the desk. The golden gaze found him, staring curiously as he spoke. 'And you are here to finish what Myan started.'

'Why would the Dragon…'

'Aye.' The Dragon spoke slowly, as if considering every word before it was said. 'It was left unfinished. And the deal must be honoured.'

This surprised Kasari; the implication was something unexpected. 'That's why you came back?'

'In part.'

But Athrin's concerns were elsewhere, revelation or otherwise. 'Then it is done?' he asked the Dragon without waiting for the answer. 'Let Lisara go.'

'That is not what she wants.'

'Yes it is.' It was time. They were so close. 'You said the deal must be honoured but you have not made one with Lisara.'

The golden gaze narrowed at Athrin, observing him carefully.

'Let her go.'

The Dragon pulled the blade from the floor and leapt from the desk. 'That is not my decision to make.'

'Athrin,' Kasari snapped, readying her weapon and tightening her grip. 'Words won't work here.'

Part of him wished she was wrong. None of their bouts against this being had gone well; he was still recovering from the aftermath of the last one. But she was right, it was time to act.

Kasari whipped her blade to the side and began walking towards the Dragon. A gentle shimmer rose up from the sharp edge. 'Honestly, I'm sick of all this.' Kasari locked her icy gaze on the Dragon and focused her full attention. 'Everyone tries to guess what you want, what you're doing and why. While you stand there with that smug look on your face, pretending it's some grand plan when you're nothing but an expired old lizard passed his due.' Tightening her grip on her weapon, she was primed for the final bout. 'And I'm sick of it, I'm sick of you. No more speeches.'

The Dragon smiled, shifting one foot to the left and into a poised stance. 'At last, we agree.'

Quicker than a flash of lightning, the two crossed swords and their fight began. The darkened office lit up with each spark as the blades met. Each parry, each strike, quicker and fiercer than the last. Athrin could only watch as the two darted around the room, furniture cleaved into pieces as collateral.

Athrin watched them as they fought. The flash of silver and steel against the backdrop of torrential rain; it was quite the surreal sight. He reached into his pocket and removed the pouch he had kept with him all this time. He unfolded the wrapping, just one corner, to see the crimson glow inside. He could almost hear it humming, as if anticipating what would come next.

The Dragon leapt over the splintered remains of a chair and hurled it at Kasari but she ducked under it and closed in with a heavy strike, pinning the Dragon to the wall. Kasari knew she had the upper hand; Lisara was no fighter. 'You chose poorly.' She kept the pressure, holding the Dragon in place, the swords scraping against each other.

'Such irony, little sorceress.'

'Shut up,' Kasari barked, firmly keeping the Dragon pinned and adjusting her footing to counter his movements. 'It's over.'

'Is that so?'

'It is.' Athrin appeared out of nowhere, taking advantage of the opportune moment Kasari had created for him. He grasped the black blade firmly in one hand and placed his other over Lisara's forehead, his thumb to her right temple. He summoned the last remnants of his strength, feeling the influence from the blood stone, and stared into the heart of the golden gaze. He could feel the grip of the blade on Lisara loosen, ever so slightly, and felt he might just be able to rip the two apart. But then, it was there, something else. It reached out from the darkness and grabbed Athrin, then pulled him in.

*

Athrin closed his eyes as he was being hauled away at an incredible speed, unable to latch onto anything. Then, with a sudden and nauseating stop, he opened his eyes.

He was in his apartment, just past the threshold. It seemed untouched, just as he had left it. But he immediately realised something was different; someone was here.

'Athrin!' a voice called out to him – a painfully familiar voice. 'You're home.'

To the left, in the kitchen, she was there. Amber. She donned that frilly pink apron he loved and washed her hands at the sink. The sudden waft of her cooking surrounded him.

Quickly drying her hands on the front of the apron, she skipped across the tiles to him, locking him in an embrace and greeting him with a smile. He was frozen, shocked. This was wrong.

'Go change, I'll have dinner ready in a little bit.' She released him and pushed him on his way, returning to the stove. 'How was your day?'

His bag was in his hand. He put it down and kicked off his shoes. Out of habit. But he said nothing, did nothing. Something felt off.

'You okay, Athrin?'

She was watching him, their eyes met. 'Yes,' he said instinctively. He lied. The apartment was colourful and decorated, just as he remembered. She always liked it to be well lit; she did not like the darkness. Slowly, he moved towards the counter to get a better look at her and what she was doing.

'Rough day?'

Quite. She had no idea. But, he couldn't remember either. What was he doing before this? Work? Yes. Work. 'No, just tired, I suppose.'

'Good.' She stirred the pot, steam drifting around her and towards Athrin. The smell filled him with comfort. 'After this, you'll be ready for another day.'

'Can't wait.' He remained there, watching her work. For some reason, it felt as if it had been such a long time since he last had the opportunity.

'Ah!' Amber flicked a grain of rice at him. It stuck to his cheek. 'You're smiling! Couldn't have been all bad then.'

'I guess not.' Something scratched at the back of his mind, something important. A feeling he could not shake. This was wrong.

With the turn of a few dials, she then moved the pot to a wooden coaster on the counter and hung the apron on the hook by the fridge. She turned to him, realising he was staring, and smiled. 'Come on, Athrin.' She swung around the counter and trotted over to him, her long auburn hair swaying back and forth. She picked the grain of rice from his cheek, then took his hands, and held them tightly. 'You can't fool me.'

No. He never could.

'I can tell when something's bothering you.'

Always. Without fail.

'I know you don't want to worry me.'

Never. He only wanted to protect her.

'But, a problem shared is a problem halved.'

That smile. Those eyes. He could never deny her.

'Tell me.'

He wanted to. He needed to. But he didn't know himself. His mind assaulted by his own thoughts – there was no clarity, only a jumbled mess with no beginning and without end. But he knew this was wrong, even if he couldn't remember why.

'Athrin?'

She touched his face. Everything within him went silent, as if by her command. The winding mess of thoughts flattened and he was suddenly at ease.

Her.

She always had that power. And slowly it all came back to him. He began to see.

'You shouldn't be here.'

He looked at her. Her hand still on his face. She smiled sadly, as if she too had realised.

'No matter how much you might want it.'

He grabbed her hand as it began to leave him, struggling to do little more but offer her a smile in return. 'I know.'

She nodded. 'Good.' Another nod. 'Then, you made something new?'

Slowly, he wrapped his arms around her. He held her so tightly and allowed himself to let the walls come down.

'I did.'

CHAPTER XX

DRAGON

Athrin opened his eyes, squinting through the bright light. He stood in a blinding white space, standing upon what appeared to be a body of water, though the surface was solid. He looked back, noting this place seemed to stretch on endlessly. Then he looked forward again, but someone else was here now, standing right in front of him.

'Why have you come?'

Athrin lost his footing and fell over. The woman before him excelled a blinding light, her hair and her dress of pure white. She looked down on him with an expression bordering on contempt and disappointment. Behind her stood a small island in this seemingly endless lake and a white tree at its centre.

'Why have you come?' she repeated.

At that moment Athrin realised the water around him held something beneath; bodies appeared to be floating just below the surface. Featureless and innumerable. He shot to his feet and circled the woman, eyeing the water cautiously. 'I am looking for something.'

The woman moved to the island to meet him, appearing to glide over the surface. She stopped nearer to the tree before facing him again. 'Tell me.'

He hesitated, considering that it was perhaps not wise to tell her what he was looking for. He had his suspicions as to who she was and her presence was dangerous.

'I mean you no harm, child.'

His eyes widened; he was sure he hadn't said anything yet.

'I was merely curious as to your intentions.'

He said nothing and fought to keep his mind blank. It seemed as if she had heard his very thoughts.

'But I see that you do not mean to bring him harm.' She drifted closer to the tree and put her hand upon it. Her hand beautifully slender, with long fingers and meticulous nails.

Athrin had seen her once before, in a vision; he knew she was the original sorceress, the source of Kasari's power and the enemy of the Dragon. But her words were a contradiction.

'You may ask, if you would prefer.'

Curiosity had gotten the better of him, but Athrin wanted to know. All he could do was ask. 'Why?'

'The whole world was against him.' She slowly ran her fingers along the smooth surface of the tree. 'Every being which drew breath, and even some that needed not, hunted him.' Her eyes grew sad as she spoke, as if remembering something painful. 'It was by his design. So I locked him away.'

'I don't understand...' Athrin muttered. This was not why he came. He felt uncomfortable here and knew the longer he lingered, the more perilous his situation. This woman before him was incredibly dangerous. But he felt he wanted to know.

'Do you know what can truly bring people together?' Her eyes found him, sharp determination within them.

There were a few things he could imagine. Create a list even. Although he couldn't pick one. None of them guaranteed it. But, she answered for him, and a sharp cold swept through him as her words reached his ears.

'Something to hate.'

Her gaze returned to the tree. 'Even sealed, and with only a sliver of his soul, he still fights to gather it.'

'Then why imprison him?'

She didn't look at him, her focus still on the tree and her hand slowly running along the surface. 'He was a man once.' Then her hand stopped and she dug her fingers and nails into the white trunk. 'Just as foolish.' Something trickled from her eyes. 'I could not stand to watch him destroy himself.'

With a quick swipe her hand left the tree and something seeped out from beneath the marks she had left. Something red. Almost like blood.

'His desire to unite a people against the coming enemy is the same force that would bring it upon them.' She turned away from Athrin. 'He could never see that.'

'Enemy?'

'Better for the world to never know.' She looked up at the branches of the tree, perhaps longingly, perhaps lovingly. 'Better for the world that you did not accept his offer.' Her head turned in Athrin's direction, her eyes consumed by a distilled wrath. 'Go now, child.'

All light suddenly faded and Athrin was left in a pitch-black void. Though, somehow, he knew with certainty that the woman and the tree were gone.

Before he could catch his breath the sea of darkness split open, perhaps gave way, to the shape of a massive beast. Fire and embers poured from its maw with every word and everything around trembled with each step as it came to stand before Athrin.

'You cannot overcome this. Lost as you are in what has passed and your refusal to accept what has changed.' The Dragon's tail uncoiled behind Athrin, cutting off any escape. 'Does it bring you comfort? Clothing yourself in those memories of a past you will not leave behind.'

Athrin could not move, could not speak. Overcome with a complete and innate fear of this tremendous creature.

'You cannot overcome this. Not with that weight you drag behind you. You cling to it so tightly you fail to realise you have already smothered it.'

The golden serpentine gaze burned a hole through Athrin's soul, peering in at everything he had denied and everything he had kept buried.

'Pretending nothing has changed will not make it so. You cannot overcome this.'

The hail of cinders over Athrin stopped as the Dragon now leered down and waited.

His heart echoed in his ears. His body ached from a concoction of injury, exertion and exhaustion. He was tired. So very tired. Athrin looked up at the Dragon, even the creature's intimidating shadow weighed down heavily upon his shoulders. But, enough was enough. He had an answer now. 'My past is important to me. It has shaped me into who I am, for better or worse. Had it not happened, or should I forget, I will be worse off for it. It is how I will know not to make the same mistakes again.'

The Dragon's glare beared down upon Athrin as it remained silent, perhaps contemplating the response, or perhaps it had gone unheard. Neither bothered Athrin; he had decided this for himself. Not because it was asked of him.

Finally, the Dragon spoke, embers weaved between sharp fangs. 'I was not speaking to you.'

Suddenly, Athrin realised he was not alone. Someone stood beside him. Lisara.

'Well?' the Dragon asked her impatiently.

She stood there, clenched fists and puffed cheeks, frustration welling up in her eyes. She looked at Athrin, with a fierce turn of her head. He flinched, reactively, habitually, feeling an instinctive pain swelling in his shin. But instead, she smiled at him. The biggest, most genuine smile he had ever seen her show. Lisara looked toward the Dragon and cleared her throat. 'I want to go home.'

The Dragon's golden eyes remained on Lisara. It could see something in her was different from before. Something, however small, had changed. 'As I said before, girl... Let go of the sword, and you will be free. No deal was made between us.'

The Dragon's tail coiled up and disappeared into the darkness as the gigantic beast turned away from them and began to recede into the void. But, before the glowing eyes faded out, they locked onto Lisara again. 'No one can do it for you.'

*

Kasari ducked under debris the Dragon had thrown at her and closed in with a heavy strike, pinning the Dragon to the wall and creating an opening. The very opening Athrin used to intervene and grasp the black blade firmly in one hand, placing his other over Lisara's forehead, his thumb to her right temple. Everything had come down to this moment.

Lisara let go. The black blade slipped from her fingers and clattered to the floor, echoing throughout the barren office as a sign. It was over.

*

Calem sat with his head in his hands, having given up arguing with the woman in the cell.

A few of his comrades ran into the room, bringing news of something that had transpired just moments ago.

Suddenly, after having been unresponsive and still for hours, Elanee looked up, as if she had heard something distinct. Life returned to her eyes and her body shook. Then, she screamed, emptied her lungs and wept, startling Calem and the others nearby.

She knew. It was over.

*

In the quiet of the office, as the relenting rain dotted against the glass, Kasari stood over the black blade. She stared at it for a time, reminiscing, considering. Finally, she reached down and lifted it off the floor. It was cold to the touch, and felt eerily familiar. She could almost hear the whispers emanating from within it.

With a flick of her wrist, a matching black scabbard appeared in her hand and she quickly sheathed the blade with a firm snap. Kasari then turned to Athrin, who sat on the floor, holding a barely conscious Lisara.

'She's been through a lot tonight,' Kasari said gently. 'You should get her looked at, and then lie low for a while.'

Lisara absentmindedly stared at her bare feet, clenching and unclenching her toes. 'Where are my damn boots?'

Athrin stood, carefully lifting Lisara in his arms. 'Kasari,' he began. 'Thank you, for everything.'

For a time, Kasari stood in silence, leading Athrin to wonder if she had heard him or not, but then she smiled and gave him a reassuring nod containing all of the gratitude she could not say. 'You should get out of here.' She motioned towards the door. 'I'll explain to the Order what the Dragon did here, and that I dealt with it.'

Athrin did not need to be told twice. With Lisara now sound asleep, he made his way to the door. But, he stopped at the threshold and turned to Kasari again. 'Kasari…'

She stopped and turned to him, puzzled by the look in his eyes.

Everything in Athrin shouted at him, forbid him from saying what he was about to say, but he couldn't help it. He wanted to know. 'Do you think you found your way?'

By all accounts, he was expecting her to throw something at him, or worse, brandish one of the sharp objects in her possession. Instead, she giggled, something he had never heard her do, and it surprised him. Then Kasari answered him with a sincere smile. 'Yes, I think so.'

*

The chaos in the city finally began to settle, and an end was in sight. Without a leader, the Order had no reason to occupy the city, and it was taken back. They would face the consequences of their leader's actions. The past night's events would change the city forever, that much was certain, but the Order was no more.

*

Athrin emptied his pockets and found the wrapped stone, noticing that the red glow had subsided and it was now inert. It was as he expected, it had helped him get through tonight's events. And now it was done.

They were home. It was just as they had left it, slightly cluttered and the faint smell of charred cookware hovered in the air. But they could not stay long. Athrin knew it was best they left the city as soon as possible.

'Got everything?' he called to the other room.

'Don't rush me, punk.'

Not yet. Affirmative.

Athrin took to strolling around the apartment. Slowly walking by all the bits and baubles and the memories attached to them. There was the sofa, which was his bed for a long time. Not far from it was the sliding door to the balcony, which was his means of escape from various situations. From out the window he could see the rain clouds begin to recede, and the early morning sun peek through the seams. It had been a long night.

'Athrin.'

Lisara had crept up behind him but did not pounce; rather, she stood there timidly.

'We're leaving because of me?'

'Yes.'

'I knew it!' She loaded a kick, aiming squarely at his shin, but he dodged it, knowing full well it was coming. 'You can't leave just because of me, idiot.' She tried to kick him again, missing a second time. 'This is your home.'

'I was joking.' Athrin barely dodged the third kick and luckily the barrage was interrupted. 'I need to get out of the city, leave all of this behind.'

'You're just saying that…'

'No,' he corrected her quickly. This was important; he had to tell her what he was thinking. 'There is too much baggage here and I want to get away from it. Maybe one day we will return.'

Still, she seemed unconvinced, and he was worried the assault on his shins would begin anew, so he made it clear. 'I want to build something new and I cannot do that here, but I have someplace else in mind. You can come along if you like.'

Lisara smiled but still did not look directly at him, sheepishly tracing the carpet stitching with her toe.

'Lisara.'

Those bright blue eyes found him. Here she was, wearing a wide smile from ear to ear. Somehow, in some way, they had managed it. Maybe he was able to help after all, yet maybe it had nothing to do with him. But more than that, now that he realised it, he was the one pulled from a deep well. She had saved him. Lisara, she was the little tornado that ripped through his stale life with reckless abandon.

'Dude...' Her smile steadily pulled into a cringe as the time went by without him saying anything. 'If you keep staring at me like that, I'll probably stab you.'

'Thank you,' he said at last, ignoring her mumbling and with a smile of his own.

'Are you smiling?!' She gasped, recoiling in apparent disgust.

His scowl returned and he looked away with a grunt, ready to walk away.

'And you thanked me!' She tugged on his shirt, anchoring him in place so that the mockery could continue. 'Are you feeling okay? Hungry? Tummy ache?'

'Regretting it already.'

'You'd only pull a face like that if you're in pain, right?' She began poking him now. 'Should I call an ambulance?'

'Let's go.' He tugged against her grip, hoping to get away from any further berating.

She grabbed his hand. Pulled him towards her. Stood on her toes. Wrapped her arms around his neck. And kissed him.

After their moment, she still hung around his neck while staring at him. 'Don't leave me behind,' she whispered with a widening smile, as sly as it always was. 'Honey-bear.'

END

Shawline Publishing Group Pty Ltd
www.shawlinepublishing.com.au

SLP

SHAWLINE
PUBLISHING
GROUP